Also by G. D. Gearino

What the Deaf-Mute Heard

G. D. Gearino

Counting Coup
A Novel

Simon & Schuster

SIMON & SCHUSTER
Rockefeller Center
1230 Avenue of the Americas
New York, NY 10020

SIMON & SCHUSTER and colophon are registered trademarks
of Simon & Schuster Inc.

Designed by Deirdre C. Amthor

Manufactured in the United States of America

10 9 8 7 6 5 4 3 2 1

Library of Congress Cataloging-in-Publication Data
Gearino, G. D. (G. Dan), 1953–
Counting coup : a novel / G. D. Gearino.
p.   cm.
I. Title.
PS3557.E214C68   1997
813'.54—dc21   97-3122
                                                       CIP

ISBN 0-684-83726-9

For the children: Meghan and Evan,
Alex and Max,
Jessica and Alicia, and Jennifer

Acknowledgments

Anyone can get lucky once, but having a second book published proves you've got some extraordinary people working on your behalf. That's indeed the case with me, and I'll sing the praises of those people here.

Jane Dystel, my literary agent, is a treasure. My initial book arrived at her office unbidden and unexpected, but she read it, liked it and sold it. She encouraged me to do a second, which you now hold, and arranged a contract for a third. Jane and her associate, Miriam Goderich, together are an author's dream: advocate, cheerleader and realist. Every writer should be so lucky.

Bob Mecoy at Simon & Schuster is an editor of subtlety, delicacy and vision. Anyone who has been in the newspaper business for twenty years, as I have, necessarily comes to understand that editors are the spawn of Satan. But any writer who works with Bob will have to reconsider that notion. There is no finer compliment. Also, he and I both were ably served by his assistant, Pete Fornatale, a man who, if the world is a fair and just place, will be no one's assistant for long.

Finally, my wife Karolyn—nurturer, friend and resident computer expert—is owed more than I know how to repay. But she says the new kitchen was a good place to start.

CHAPTER ONE

The toothless, fat kid died Sunday.

You probably remember him. Perhaps you were on a city bus one morning when he climbed aboard and stood in the front, preaching the gospel in earnest tones and stepping aside politely at each stop to let new riders aboard. Or maybe you saw him on the sidewalk one day as he sat on the curb to enjoy a typical meal of take-out fried chicken and three or four bananas, watching in awe as he gobbled away happily. The fat kid was a two-fisted eater, but generous. Chances are, he offered you a drumstick. I'll bet you declined.

Maybe you saw him stop somebody one day to shake hands. He did that a lot. He made a little ritual of it, introducing himself to two people every day, one in the morning and one in the afternoon. The lucky ones got the morning shift, because after lunch his hand was sure to be slick with chicken grease. He wasn't subtle about it—you could see him a half-block away peering into faces trying to decide who to stop and meet—and most people were alert enough to duck into a store or cross to the other side. I did, countless times.

But he made his quota every day. Two people a day, week in and week out, for the several years of his short career. By my estimate, he probably introduced himself to 4,000 people. So why did so few people know his name?

Let me answer a question with a question: Who wants to be pals with a retarded, ungainly, toothless, beefy kid who rides buses around all day and pesters you about Jesus?

It doesn't matter now, anyway. He died of a brain tumor, so he won't be shaking hands and preaching on buses anymore. But I learned a few things about the toothless, fat kid in recent days that I'd like to tell you.

His name was Benjamin Lee Woodward, Jr., and he was 23 years old. He lived with his widowed mother in Barrington Heights, which isn't really high at all. In fact, it's a place where all the runoff seems to end up after a hard rain, flooding yards and filling ditches. Benny's mother says the rain indirectly caused him to be the way he was. When he was little, he fell into an open storm sewer drain after a hard rain and nearly drowned, she says. He was never right after that, she says.

Yeah, maybe, says Barrington police Sgt. Monroe Finch. But he also remembers being called to Barrington Memorial Hospital one evening after one of her boyfriend's titanic, drunken rages. Little Benny was there, a five-year-old with an old brawler's bruises: a black eye, an ear that looked like someone had tried to twist it off, and eyes with pupils in two different sizes, a sure sign of brain trauma.

No charges were filed, Finch remembers. Benny's mom said he fell down the steps, and besides, this was back when children were hurt and not seen. Finch made it a point after that to stop by the Woodward household occasionally to check on Benny. He never found the youngster in that sort of shape again, but what was done was done.

Benny was in a special class for a while, long enough to learn to read a bit. And at some point—it's not clear when—he heard about Jesus. They became great pals.

Benny made it his life's work to tell as many people as possible about Jesus. Because I was particularly deft at avoiding both of them, I never heard Benny's pitch. But the drivers of

*Barrington's buses, where Benny did most of his preaching,
heard it often.*

*"He would stand in the front, next to me, with the Bible in
one hand, and wave and gesture like the preachers do on television," says driver Roland Fellows. "I think he must have
watched them a lot. Also, he would pretend to refer to the
Bible for a certain passage. But I could see he didn't have it
open to the right page. And he mixed up the words sometimes.
You know the part in John that says, 'God so loved the world
He gave His only begotten son'? Well, Benny would always say
'His only forgotten son.' I tried to help him out with it once,
but he couldn't seem to get his tongue wrapped around it."*

*Another driver simply says this: "He was the sweetest hu-
man being you'd ever meet."*

*Benny may have had a friend in Jesus, but the drivers became
his family. They saw something special in him that eluded people like me. They chipped in and bought him a coat for Christmas. They made sure he always had a little money to give the
Colonel for chicken. And finally, they carried his coffin.*

*The toothless, fat kid was dropped in the ground Tuesday,
buried with the Bible he misquoted from so often. I attended
the service. Afterwards, I went to the drivers' lounge at the municipal bus depot, where Benny's only friends held a wake for
him. They toasted his life with soft drinks, told their best stories about him and had lunch.*

Chicken and bananas never tasted so good.

That's what I do. Every Tuesday, Thursday and Sunday, I give
you a reason to pick up the morning newspaper. I'll take 750
words or so and arrange them this way or that, and make sure
that when you come to the end, I have you in my hand. Some
mornings I'll leave you snickering, some mornings I'll leave you
outraged, and some mornings I'll leave you dropping tears into
your Cheerios.

I don't worry about objectivity, fairness, balance or all the other things that journalists promise to honor. If you want a recitation of the facts, go to the front page. If you want the issues weighed, measured and debated, turn to that wasteland called the editorial pages. Don't ask me to make the picture clear for you. That's somebody else's role. I'm the storyteller, wielder of the gut punch and the fond caress. If in the course of the morning I've angered a politician, offended a few churchgoers, enraged a Rotarian and made an editor squirm and regret the moment he ever gave me this job, then it's a successful day.

I am a creature of twentieth-century American journalism. I am what it invented to battle that strange, twilight coupling of television and ignorance. There was a time when the printed word was how people informed themselves. It was how we were led to our outrage or joy or compassion, whatever the moment called for. Untold millions of us every morning turned to the page that carried H. L. Mencken or Damon Runyon or, later, Jimmy Breslin. There, we found more nuance and subtlety and wisdom about the world, sometimes in a single sentence, than television can deliver in an hour.

But television is the perfect lover for an impatient world: It gives us release without asking us to work for it. Newspapers are now like the stereotype of the first wife—smart and clever as ever, but increasingly shrill as her looks fade and resentment over the livelier, younger competitor builds. These days, too many people drop their quarter into the newspaper box only because their car just died and they need to see who's got another one to be had for a few hundred dollars; or because it's Monday morning, and the standings in the fantasy football league have to be adjusted; or because layoffs are coming at the plant and it's time to see what other jobs are out there.

So newspaper editors need me to stack the words, this way or that. We spend two minutes together three days a week, and we arrive at the end each time either friends or enemies. It's nice if you like me, but I'd prefer that you didn't. I don't want the responsibility of your affection. I've never been all that happy with myself, so it makes me uneasy when others profess to be. Oh, I'll accept your compliment with a grateful smile, and I'll dash off a note in acknowledgment of your letter. I even gave an autograph once, to a drunk in a bar who insisted I sign a cocktail napkin. But loathing is better: It's much less intrusive, yet just as loyal.

■

Justice tripped me up.

I should have known better. Justice is capricious and treacherous, as anyone who sees its application knows. It cannot be wrought. A wrong is like an iceberg, with most of its mass concealed from sight, and it is the foolish man who seeks to apply justice to what he can see. I knew that.

I also knew from the beginning that truth is likewise elusive. I knew the truth is shaded a thousand different ways, shaped and fitted ever so slightly by whoever held it at the moment before it was handed back to me with the earnest plea: "Just print the truth."

God, how many times did someone call me, write me, stop me on the street to demand that I just tell the truth? How many times did I hear this profoundly impossible request? Tell the truth? I'd love to. I'd love to be able to sort through a dozen different accounts of the same event and extract the truth. I want desperately to plow through court records, accounting statements, police reports or council minutes and be confident that everything was transcribed perfectly and precisely, with no misplaced numbers or transposed words. I've tried to forget that a countless number of the "facts" drummed into me by a parade of teachers, ministers and relatives have been contradicted by more contemporary ideas offered up in a we-really-know-for-sure-this-time tone. Anyone who thinks the truth can be found is a fool, a naive, trusting, dangerous fool. I knew that. But when the time came for me to dispense justice, I forgot it. My foolishness cost me my job and cost my publisher millions of dollars.

Yes, I'm actually on the sidelines now. No longer do I arrange the words this way and that. When I finally learned my lesson, I learned it a little too well, and I now can find certainty only in the smallest places and routines. But even if I wanted back in the game, and I don't, no one would have me. My two failures were high-profile affairs, much discussed and debated. The first was, perversely, a triumph in the beginning, making me a valued commodity to be wooed by editors everywhere. But the second was unforgivable to those very same people, making me an outcast.

■

But this is not a story about journalism. It takes place in and around newspapers, but it's really the tale of one person who knew something and another who had to learn it. That thing is this: God help you if you ever get a second chance.

CHAPTER TWO

Despite much evidence to the contrary, I have always considered myself rootless. True, I grew up in my ancestral home and worked in a nearby town until I was in my mid-thirties. It's also true that I lived among people who'd known me since my birth; some of them had known my mother since her birth, and a few of the oldest ones had known even my grandfather since his birth. Had I been allowed to venture that far as a child, I could have walked through the woods behind my house for a mile or so, crossed the highway and continued for another mile until I came to a church graveyard filled with my forebears, including a great-great grandfather who'd left an arm somewhere on the ground during the second battle of Manassas and an uncle two generations back who'd served a term in the state legislature.

So "rootless" isn't the first word that comes to mind when you learn of my circumstance. If anything, you'd think I would be head of the local chapter of the Sons of the Confederacy, spending my time earnestly explaining that the war wasn't about slavery and that no Son has anything but love for his black brothers, at least those who behave themselves and don't whine every time they see the rebel flag.

But I was almost literally no one's son. For as long as I can remember, I've had an outsider's sensibility. Life has always seemed like an improvisational theater, where everyone except me meets offstage somewhere to go over their routines and nail down their timing and delivery. Then, when everything is worked out, I arrive onstage and suddenly find myself in the middle of other people's lives. Sometimes the other actors are forgiving and understanding as I blunder through my role, but other times they're impatient and resentful, making sure I understand that I don't really belong among them. At the end of each day, everyone else retires to those secret places in the rear of the stage while I trudge back to my seat to await the next raising of the curtain.

I grew up in a place called Doralee. It's the last town that can claim to be in Georgia before U.S. 29 hits the South Carolina line. Down the road in the other direction is Royston, which—as you're reminded the moment you hit the city limits—was home to baseball great Ty Cobb. My grandfather claimed to have played baseball against Cobb one time, which means that on one memorable afternoon in the early 1900s, on some remote, dusty Southern ball field, the world achieved a critical mass of prick.

I won't pretend I have no idea what caused my sense of rootlessness, though. My father was a Yankee and the grandson of Jewish immigrants. His own father, for reasons long since lost to history, had shunned his faith and family, anglicized his name and married an Irish woman from Hell's Kitchen. That union produced one child, my father, who himself continued this legacy of cultural confusion by marrying a rural-born, timid Southern girl he encountered in a train station. He was a soldier at the time, traveling from a boot camp in Alabama to his first posting, and my mother was working as a volunteer in the train depot in Atlanta, one of the army of young women who served soft drinks and cookies to servicemen at countless public places. It was 1944, and the fevered wartime atmosphere had already prompted the first of my mother's two sole acts of rebellion in her life: Against my grandfather's wishes, she had accepted a cousin's offer of room and board in Atlanta for a summer of girlish adventure.

Then one afternoon, she served a refreshment to a tall, dark-eyed infantryman who lingered by her table for an hour before reluctantly running at the last moment to catch his train. A few moments later, he was back.

"People are going to be shooting at me in a few weeks," he said. "If I'm going to die, I'd like to at least know your name."

I heard this story from my mother dozens of times, and listening to her languid, honeyed accent, I could understand what made my father return to her table. Her voice has always been her best feature, a slow drawl that within minutes doubtless had my father dreaming of verandas and sloe gin and the feel of her breath in his ear on warm, humid nights.

Ironically, her voice was completely at odds with her character. The person my father must have believed was confident, sensual and adventurous—and what else could he think of a fetching girl, barely out of high school, who answered a strange soldier's come-on with a sly look and this retort: "If my daddy saw the way you're looking at me, he wouldn't wait a few weeks"—was in fact insecure and helpless. What he must have assumed was a barely banked fire of passion was instead a single flicker, a show of verve that lasted only the two weeks they spent together.

Perhaps my father's boldness also was uncharacteristic; I don't know. He was somehow able to arrange for the army to do without him long enough to court my mother and prompt her second, and last, act of rebellion. They were married ten days after meeting in the train station, despite my grandfather's threats and ultimate boycott of the service. Sometime in the following few days, the seed that would become me was planted.

After my father left to report for duty, my mother reverted to form. My grandfather told her it wasn't proper for a married woman to flaunt her charms around soldiers, so she stopped volunteering. He then told her it wasn't right to just hang around Atlanta living off her cousin's largesse, so she moved back to Doralee. When my fetal presence became known, he told her folks would assume she was a grass widow and it wasn't much better to say she was a Yankee's wife, so she should keep out of sight, which meant my mother spent her pregnancy fanning herself on the porch and waiting for letters from my father, sinking deeper into that peculiar darkness of helplessness from which she never really emerged. And when the telegram came saying he was dead, my grandfather told her that was that, she could pack up those letters now and put them away and get on with life.

But I was the one bit of evidence of my mother's summer of rebellion that couldn't be packed away. I was born in the summer of 1945 after a twenty-nine-hour labor that left my mother barely conscious the following day. So it fell to my grandfather to see that the birth certificate was filled out. From one of the letters, he got the proper spelling of my father's name: Allen Beckman of New York City. In the place for my mother's name, he listed them all: Vivian Collie Roseen Beckman of Doralee, Georgia. Her last name was written in cramped, tight letters, as if he hadn't planned to include it, but added it later at someone's prompting.

In the space for my name, my grandfather wrote "Thaddeus Stevens Beckman." A few days afterward, my mother protested that it wasn't the name she'd wanted for me, but she took no step to correct it. I doubt my grandfather would have let her, anyway. He was enchanted with his own cleverness. "A good Yankee name for a Yankee's son," he said, using a phrase I heard countless times throughout my life and grew to detest.

■

We made an odd little family.

There were just the three of us. My grandmother had died when my mother was young, and no one talked much about her: my grandfather because he was still clearly annoyed years later to have been given no son and left with a girl to raise; my mother because she had so few memories of her; and me because every question about her was answered only with a shrug or a grunt.

My grandfather worked as a foreman in a cotton mill. The company provided homes for many of its workers in a village on the edge of Doralee, but my grandfather preferred to live a couple of miles outside of town. He fancied himself a farmer, and kept a garden on one side of the house and a yearling in the pasture on the other. In the fall, my mother put the garden into jars, and in the winter the yearling was confined to the barn, where I fed him grain and meal to fatten him. When I was younger, they were my pets. I named each of them, and would chatter at them all winter, feeding them corncobs by hand and assigning to them all sorts of personality traits and moods.

"Domino's feeling a little peevish," I said one day. I was six, and "peevish" was a word I'd just learned and was using a lot. I didn't have its meaning down exactly, and tended to use it mostly when referring to inanimate objects: I couldn't tie my shoes because the laces were peevish, for instance.

"How do you know?" my mother asked.

"He's not eating much," I said. "Maybe his food is peevish."

"You keep that cow fed," my grandfather said. "I need that freezer locker filled."

"What?" I said, confused. I hadn't yet made the connection between the disappearance of my pets and the meat that filled the locker my grandfather rented in town.

"You said you wouldn't tell him," my mother said.

"You mean he doesn't know?" my grandfather asked in mock surprise. He turned his attention back to me. "Son, you've got the tastiest pets in town. But it's a good thing you ain't partial to dogs. I've never had much of a taste for them."

I started to cry and my mother came over to hug me. After a moment, my grandfather waved her off.

"Leave him be. God knows you don't need to make him any softer."

As always, my mother did what she was told.

■

I was Collie's boy. On the occasional trip into Doralee with my grandfather, or on the rare occasion someone came to visit, that's how I was always introduced. Around the house, he called me "son" or "boy." Only my mother called me by name.

Our neighbors took their cue from him. I was treated with a well-mannered detachment in town and in school, the sort of polite acknowledgment one makes of distant relatives or long-term guests. Aside from my teachers, only one adult talked to me very much. He owned a store on the crossroads corner a half-mile from my grandfather's house.

It was the rural South's version of the convenience store, a place where you could get gas, cigarettes, bread, twine, credit and gossip. The owner's name was Almo Hardy, and he was a cheery fellow with one droopy eyelid that made it seem like he was always winking. Part of the forefinger on his right hand was missing, too, severed at the first knuckle and puckered at the tip, where the skin had grown together. I was fascinated with his finger, and frequently asked him how he'd lost it. The answer changed every time.

"A lawn mower cut it off," he said one day. There was no one else in the store, and I felt free to lean against the front counter and nurse my bottled chocolate drink like the men did.

"You stuck your hand under the lawn mower?" I asked.

"Nah. I was napping in the yard when it started up by itself. Ran over my hand before I woke up."

At other times, he told me a pig had bitten it off, that he'd accidentally shot it off while squirrel hunting, and that his daddy cut it off as punishment for lying. Each tale was delivered with a straight face and elaborate detail, and each featured some malevolent force that struck with inexplicable violence. He always answered my follow-up questions earnestly, and never failed to register surprise when, at the end, I said, "Aw, I don't believe that."

"Wait a minute. You think I'm making this up?" he would ask. "I may have to reconsider your credit situation."

Indeed, I had a tab at Almo's store. He'd created it for me not long after my range—the amount of territory I was allowed to cover on foot or on my bike—had been extended to the store. I'd visited often enough with my grandfather, of course, but it wasn't until it became apparent late one afternoon that we didn't have enough milk to last until morning that I was allowed to walk down the road to the store by myself. I was nine years old, and this was an exciting new addition to my map of the world.

I took a half-gallon of milk to the counter, but then found myself pulled into the irresistible orbit of the ice cream freezer. It was a large chest squatting on the floor next to the cash register, a boxy temptress with sliding glass doors through which her delights beckoned: Eskimo pies, Popsicles, ice cream sandwiches and cups of sherbet with little wooden spoons taped to their sides. In one corner was a box full of various candy bars, frozen to a brick-hard consistency to suit some customers' tastes. I knew the location of everything by heart, but was rarely allowed to claim one; my grandfather was not the sort who bought treats, and had in fact once lectured Almo about the mercenary placement of the freezer so close to the counter.

I looked for a long moment at the orderly stacks, then on impulse grabbed a Popsicle and laid it on the counter next to the milk. Almo reached for the box that sat next to the register and walked his fingers along the spines of the dozens of palm-sized notebooks it contained until he found one that carried my grandfather's name. He withdrew it, licked his pencil and entered the price of the milk and Popsicle.

"Your grandpa say it's okay to have that?" he asked casually as he wrote.

"It's okay," I said. I had already begun to unwrap the Popsicle, taking care to pull the paper away gingerly lest it rip and leave a bit of frozen wrapper bonded to the bar.

Almo pressed the point. "It's pretty close to dinnertime. You sure?"

I nodded. Almo closed the notebook and returned it to the box. "If you say so," he said, sounding skeptical.

I went straight home with the milk, eating as I walked and discarding the evidence in the ditch. My diligence was rewarded with an approving nod from my grandfather, and when another trip to the store became necessary a few days later—for cigarettes this time—I again was drafted. I treated myself to an ice cream sandwich that day.

The process repeated itself two more times before my grandfather went to settle his tab with Almo. My grandfather had been paid that day, and as was his routine, he visited the various merchants who extended him credit to bring his debts up to date. He usually took me with him, partly for company but mostly because I think he suspected that my Jewish blood, even diluted as it was, lent itself to financial trickery; he believed it was good for me to see that a man settled his obligations quickly and completely.

First we stopped at the store in the mill village, where my grandfather paid the monthly fee for the box he rented at the post office annex there. Then we went to the feed store and paid for the hundred-pound sack of grain that my yearling had already worked halfway through. Next was the finance company, to make the payment on his car, then the electric cooperative and the fuel-oil company. Our last stop, just before we made the turn for home, was Almo's.

Somehow, in the way the young can be blind to consequences, I had ignored the inevitable reckoning. I knew my grandfather scrutinized his bills carefully. How could I have been so reckless?

I sat in the car as he went in. "Ain't you getting out?" he asked. I shook my head.

It didn't take long. A few moments later, he stepped out of the store and gave a come-here wave. When I went inside, I saw that the account book was open on the counter between them.

"It seems you've taken some liberties with my finances," my grandfather said with a menacing formality.

"Yes, sir, I guess so," I said.

"Do you have any money to pay Mr. Hardy?" he asked.

"Yes, sir, at home," I said. Indeed, I'd hoarded some coins, which were stashed in a cigar box along with my other treasures: a .22-caliber bullet I'd found on the ground, the rattle from a rattlesnake my grandfather had killed in the barn, a handful of baseball cards, some marbles, a whistle and a picture of some second-tier movie star that had come in a Christmas gift wallet and that I imagined looked like my father.

"Then you'll need to come back this afternoon and settle up," he said. "And you'll have to be punished."

Almo spoke for the first time. "Henry, this is probably my fault."

My grandfather turned back to him. "Oh?"

"I told him to help himself to a treat. You never minded when Collie did it when she was little, so I thought it was okay."

"That was different. I could trust Collie," my grandfather said.

The words were harsh even for him. "C'mon, he's a good kid," Almo said.

"He'll become one someday," my grandfather said, "as long as people like you don't get in the way."

Almo said nothing more, silently giving my grandfather the change from his ten-dollar bill—after subtracting my charges from the amount due—and noting the transaction in the account book. Twenty minutes later, I was back with the coins from my cigar box.

"Keep your money," Almo said when I laid them on the counter.

I thought he was mad at me, even though he'd chosen to jump in with the lie about encouraging me to help myself. "I'm sorry about this," I said.

"It ain't your fault. But I'll tell you what we do. How 'bout if I set up your own account book?"

He reached under the counter, withdrew a clean spiral notebook and wrote my name on the cover. He entered my balance due, fifty-five cents, and the date, then closed it and stored it in the box containing the other account books.

"There we go," he said.

"But I still have to pay you," I said.

"You can work it off. Why don't you start by picking up outside?"

In a way, I suppose my story began that day. There is, indeed, a certain symmetry: Until then, I had lived on life's fringe, my world defined exclusively by my grandfather. But the more time I spent at Almo's store—the more I came to know other men, hear them talk, listen to the rhythm and cadence of their stories—the more I came to understand my place in life. I may have been a fatherless half-breed, but I learned that working hard, keeping your mouth shut and remembering everything you see and hear made up for a lot. Now, over forty years later, I have returned to the fringe. Instead of a rural store, I sit on a fishing pier that juts away from a coastal Georgia island. But I still listen to older men talk, the retirees in baseball caps who tend crab nets and surreptitiously sip beer as they form their lawn chairs into loose clumps and relive their better days. Age has stiffened their fingers, made them vulnerable to the waving claws, so I pluck the crabs from their nets when a catch is made. Once again, I'm a good lad: quiet, helpful and attentive.

■

Even as I began to edge away from my grandfather's world, my mother retreated into it.

My memory is cruel toward her. She is aged and helpless now, tended to by strangers and allowed to dress up only on holidays or the rare days I visit. She's barely seventy, but when the spirit leaves, the body ages quickly. And it's clear to me now, as I seek to entice my own spirit to return, that hers left early and permanently.

I don't remember her as a young woman. I was born a month after her nineteenth birthday, and at the time of my earliest memories she wasn't even twenty-five years old. Yet the face that comes to me as I think back is that of a middle-aged woman, with sad eyes, loose skin, and teeth and fingertips stained by an endless parade of cigarettes. Her clothes were added as the seasons cooled, so that by midwinter sweaters and socks were layered over one another, peeled off only for the occasional bath and reassembled randomly. She sometimes went days without speaking, preparing our meals and tending to the house in dead silence; other times she was chatty and funny, serving dinner with a flourish and talking back to the radio.

But bizarre behavior wasn't her exclusive domain. I used to hear my grandfather creeping around the house at night, would listen to his footsteps in the hall outside my bedroom, or hear them creaking up the steps as he climbed the staircase. Sometimes the footsteps would trail off toward his bedroom, and I would hear them no more after his door closed. Other times the footsteps just stopped somewhere in the hall, as if he were listening for something that only he could hear.

Once I watched through slitted eyes as he opened the door to my room and looked at me for a moment before withdrawing and closing the door. I remember being disoriented the next morning, unsure that it had actually happened: Had I been awake when he opened the door but only pretended to be asleep? Or had I actually been asleep but dreaming that I was awake? Another time the footsteps seemed to lead to my mother's bedroom, and I thought I could hear them talking. I fretted that they were talking about me. I had an irrational fear that I would be carted to the orphanage someday, that my grandfather would simply declare that it would be best to house me with the other strays, so it worried me to hear them talking privately.

One day we suddenly left. I was six or seven at the time, and I remember a trip to Atlanta on a bus and a blur of nights spent sleeping on cots on someone's back porch. There were several phone conversations that carried a tone of negotiation, held only when that strange house was empty but for the two of us, and a couple of times my mother held me as she cried. Then there was a bus trip back to Doralee, where my grandfather met us at the depot, somehow managing to look angry and wary and relieved all at the same time.

"I don't mean any harm, you know," he said.

"You just remember what we talked about," my mother replied with a rare show of verve. They both seemed to be taking care to not give me a clue as to what had happened.

We walked in silence to his car and returned home. Things were easy between them for a while, but they eventually settled back into their roles, the ruler and the ruled. Aside from the occasional trip around town, I don't recall that my mother ever left the house again during my childhood.

■

My grandfather was cold, brutal and abusive, while my mother was merely meek and helpless. Naturally, I hated her more.

I left as soon as I could. I enrolled at the university, then spent my first year there scrounging for financial aid. I also discovered that the corporation which owned the mill where my grandfather worked had a scholarship program, so I obtained an application and forged his signature. It netted me $1,000 and a threat when he found out.

"That's the Jew in you," my grandfather said. "Do it again and I'll have you arrested."

Later, while he was away, my mother offered a bit of comfort. "I'd have done the same thing. He's not going to give you anything."

I shrugged. I knew where this was going, as it had countless times before.

"At least you have a chance. I'm stuck here."

Early on, I'd encouraged her to have strength. Later, I would make soothing noises, remarkable only for their insincerity. But at that moment, I said nothing, refusing to feed what I had come to see as an addiction to pity. We sat in silence for a few long moments before she tried again.

"I wish I were younger. I'd do something with my life."

I kissed her forehead and left. The next day I wrote to the president of the company that employed my grandfather, thanking him not only for the scholarship but also for being tolerant of my grandfather's rabidly pro-union sentiment. It takes a large-hearted company to embrace such a diversity of viewpoints, I noted.

A few weeks later, my grandfather was busted down from his foreman's job and returned to the machine he'd left years before. No reason was given, my mother reported, other than the company had suddenly decided he wasn't "management material."

■

Given a mystery to chew over, almost no one will conclude something is an accident. They'll add supposition and speculation until the most mundane inconsistency evolves into something profound and unique. As I'd grown, my curiosity about my father's family had developed in lockstep with my grandfather's disdain. I had my mother's tale of their meeting, of course, and a stealthy, committed rummaging of the house had turned up the handful of letters he'd written before his death. But they contained nothing about his background, suggesting little else beyond his clear desire to occupy her bed again as soon as possible. So it was left to my imagination to create a history for him, and me, and over time that history became an epic. When a child—especially a lonely one with an imagination fueled by countless adventure books and detective stories—turns his attention to a mystery, he'll always conclude it's a textbook case of destiny thwarted.

But epics seem to suffer in the cold light of reality. During the spring break of my second year in college, I impulsively caught a bus to New York. When I arrived at the Port Authority bus terminal, I searched the bank of pay telephones until I found one that still had a phone book attached. Among the pages of Smiths and Browns, there was only one Beckman. I wrote down the address, then spent a half-hour figuring out where it was and how to get there.

I got off the subway in the Village and pushed my way toward the address. It was a warm day, perhaps the first of the season there, and the sidewalks were full. I heard a number of different languages, and even the English seemed to be accented in countless ways; my own tongue thickened the two times I asked directions, making me sound like I'd just stepped off the turnip truck.

The address, when I finally found it, turned out to be a decaying apartment building near Washington Square. It was on a narrow street, a half-block from the main thoroughfare, and in the quiet I could hear my footsteps echo. There was an intercom with ten buttons to the side of the building's heavy glass door, but none of the buttons was marked. Inside, however, I could see a row of mailboxes with names on them, and when I pulled on the door, it opened. I stepped into the foyer.

The smell was horrible. Just outside one of the two ground-floor apartments, someone had set out a bag of garbage, and its soggy bottom had split and spilled crap all over the hallway floor. There was also the rank odor of something noxious cooking. Somewhere the volume on a television was turned up way too high.

I examined the mailboxes. Three of them carried no name, and the other seven were a mishmash of ethnicities. The last one, marked as apartment 5-B, was labeled "Beckman."

There was no elevator, so I climbed to the building's top floor. One of the two doors at the top of the stairs was unmarked, while the other was labeled 5-A. I knocked on the blank door. Even then, my powers of deduction were awesome.

I heard someone inside shuffle toward the door, but it didn't open. "Who is it?" a woman's voice said.

"Mrs. Beckman?" I asked.

"Whaddya want?"

"Is this where Ira Beckman lives?" The phone book I'd consulted an hour earlier had listed only a man's name. If this was my grandmother, I didn't even know how to address her.

"There ain't no Ira Beckman," the woman said. "He's dead."

"Are you Mrs. Beckman?"

"Whaddya want?" she repeated.

I hadn't given this part much thought. What was I supposed to say—"Hello, Granny, it's me, your beloved grandson, here for a little apple pie in your warm, homey kitchen. Take off that apron and give me a hug"?

I blurted out the first thing that came to mind: "U.S. census. I just need to ask a couple of questions."

The door opened a few inches, as far as the chain would stretch. A haggard, elderly woman peered out, blinking several times as if she'd just come out into sunlight, even though the hall was dim. Despite the warm weather, she wore a sweater over a faded print dress, and the buttons on her sweater were mismatched with the holes, leaving one long tail hanging down in front. Behind her, in the small slice of the apartment I could see beyond the door, was a table with a hot plate, a pan crusted with what looked like old food, and a half-empty liquor bottle. Her breath was boozy.

"Yeah?" she said.

"So Mr. Ira Beckman is deceased?" I said, trying to sound official.

"That's right."

"And your name is . . . ?"

"Mrs. Ira Beckman."

I hoped her stupidity wasn't genetic. "No, I mean your given name."

"Oh. Eileen Beckman."

"Thank you. Do you have any children, Mrs. Beckman?"

She hesitated, then said, "No."

"I'm sorry. They teach us to ask these questions better," I said, slipping into the role. She hadn't noticed, or didn't care, that I had no identification or forms to fill out. "Have you ever had children?"

She hesitated again before answering. "Yes, a son. He died in the war."

Behind her, a cat leaped up to the table and began nibbling on the food in the pan. "I see. Was he married? Have children?"

"I don't know. We sort of lost touch."

"What was his name?"

"Allen." She blinked several times again and her eyes seemed to focus. "What's this all about? I ain't read about no census."

"We have to update the information periodically," I said.

"Well, I'm through talking," she said, shutting the door. From inside, I heard her say "Shoo!" then there was the sound of the bottle breaking on the floor. "Goddamn you," she said.

She yanked the door open again. "Don't they pay for help-ing with the census?" she said. She didn't seem surprised that I was still standing there.

"Uh, not normally."

"Well, they should," she said, and waited expectantly.

I had enough money for the bus trip home, and not much more. Still, I reached into my wallet and gave her $10. She took it without a word and shut the door again.

■

I went to a nearby bar and spent the rest of the afternoon getting drunk, marveling that the bartender hadn't asked me to prove I was old enough for this ritualistic sacrifice of brain cells. Perhaps my unhappiness gave me gravity. I had the sense that something irretrievable was gone, that I had banked too much on a notion that was now revealed as groundless and foolish. My unhappiness, of course, was as fanciful as my original longing had been for something epically satisfying. I had wanted too much, so naturally I felt my disappointment was tragically poignant. But both ends of the process were inflated by youthful desire. I had known for a long time that I was alone in the world, yet I'd fashioned an edifice of belonging from a few stray facts and a wealth of need for it. Then, when reality confirmed what circumstance already had suggested, my disappointment was as wildly out of proportion as my hopes had been. I was a chump, and I vowed never to be one again.

Shortly after dark, I walked the whole way back to the Port Authority terminal and slept sitting up on a bench, waking at 3 A.M. with a headache and a stiff neck. I figured I would have to hitchhike most of the way home, so I fortified myself with a big breakfast and several cups of coffee, then spent what little money I had left on a bus ticket to Philadelphia, the longest distance I could afford. At a stop somewhere in rural New Jersey, though, I got off the bus, realizing that I was more likely to find a ride alongside the highway than from some inner-city depot.

It worked. The first ride came almost immediately, from an elderly gentleman who spent several hours helping me get right

with Jesus before dropping me off just past Baltimore. The next
ride, on a moving van hauling someone's household, took me
to Richmond, Virginia. The last ride came from a group of
Jewish students from Hofstra University heading to Florida for
spring break. There were four of them, two men and two
women, arranged in the car like old married couples: the men
in the front, the women in the back. I squeezed into the middle
of the backseat.

The women were sweet and brazen and funny, sharing their
sandwiches and making a good-natured mockery of my accent.
The relationships between the four of them weren't clear, but
the men seemed to be annoyed by the attention being paid to
me by the women.

"So what's it like being a Southern boy?" the driver asked at
one point.

"It's the greatest thing in the world," I said.

"What's so great about it?"

"Well, what's better than being white, male and Southern?"

"How about being a decent human being?"

"Yeah, maybe," I said. "But I wouldn't know. I've never met
one."

The other man turned in the seat to address me directly. "So
what do you boys do for entertainment? I mean, when you're
not beating colored people?"

"You want an honest answer?"

"Yeah," he said.

"We think up new ways to get rid of the bodies of civil rights
workers," I said.

We rode in silence for a few minutes until someone turned
on the car radio. They then spent the next hour cruising the
dial, seeking out country music stations and howling with
laughter at the songs and the voices. By the time they let me out
of the car at a highway crossroads they were a unit again, and
the rapport I'd had with the women early on was gone.

"Thanks for the ride," I said as I got out.

One of the men leaned out of the passenger-side window and offered a bit of advice: "Treat your coloreds better, Billy Bob. Or they might slip into the plantation house one night and cut your throat." The others smirked as the car pulled away.

I wasn't one of them; they'd made that clear. But the moment they drove off, leaving me at that remote crossroads near Doralee, I became one of them again: The Yankee. The Jew. Collie's boy.

I turned my back toward home and stuck my thumb out one more time.

CHAPTER THREE

A tornado at night is nature's greatest treachery.

First comes the darkness, as it does at the end of every day, to lull us with the comfort of the routine. Then comes a hard rain drumming on roofs and windows, to lull us to sleep as we lie snug and dry in the embrace of our homes. It is easy, in those moments before sleep, to see nature as a volatile but essentially benign force: Its moisture nurtures our crops and its winds strip away from the trees that which is dead or soon to be. The noise and drama just beyond the bedroom wall never intrude.

But one time, it does.

"I had just rolled over to look at the clock when the roof went flying off," said Rowena Hallman. "Everything on Roy's side of the room went sailing up and was gone. There was a big dresser with a mirror, took three of us to horse it into the room when we moved. Well, that thing went up like someone put rocket motors under it. But nothing happened to the stuff near me. There's a picture of me with my granny, from when I was just a baby, sitting on a table next to the bed and it didn't even get tipped over. And another weird thing. The bedspread got blown away, and the wind pulled the sheets right out from under us. I remember laying there on the bare mattress wishing I'd put pajamas on or something."

Rowena and Roy used to live in a three-bedroom wood-frame home just off Altahatchee Road. Around them were neighbors and friends who lived in similar homes scattered about on one-acre lots. Most of them are just one generation away from the farm, and all of them have a need for enough land for at least a garden and maybe a few chickens.

None of them live there anymore. They were evicted Sunday night in the rudest fashion.

"It takes longer to tell about it than it took for it to happen," Rowena said. "One second I'm asleep, then the next second my house is being wrecked while I lay in bed. And a second after that, everything's quiet again."

Sometimes you hear of tornadoes that hopscotch through an area, destroying some homes but hurtling over others. That didn't happen here. Sixteen homes sitting on 16 adjoining plots of land were destroyed. The last of them belonged to Leon Lettner, whose home sits near the edge of the Ravine, Soque County's answer to the Grand Canyon. There are no homes beyond his, and it almost seems as if the tornado was a malevolent, thinking force: It didn't lift its deadly trunk until the last home had been destroyed.

"On one side of the house, you can see clear through to Barrington now," Leon said. "Used to be nothing but trees. But on the other side, there ain't a single tree down. He got done with my house, he just pulled up and went on his way."

Houses weren't the only casualties. There are 23 chickens unaccounted for, five barns down, a lawn tractor squashed almost flat under a downed tree, and countless tomatoes disappeared from one garden, deposited God-knows-where by a wind that stripped the fruit but curiously left the vines intact, still tied to their stakes.

And for a while, it seemed that Lady was a casualty.

Lady is a four-year-old English setter, a happy and faithful friend with an uncanny nose for birds. She was the runt of a litter and was given to Major Johnson by a friend who couldn't

*sell her and wouldn't keep her. So Major, who's as soft on dogs
as he is merciless on birds, adopted Lady and took her in the
field with Duke, his first-string pointer, in hopes that the pup
would pick up a few lessons from an old pro.*

*Poor Duke. He lost his starting job before the middle of bird
season. Lady ran circles around him, finding birds in thickets
that Duke had dismissed only moments before and leaving him
panting as she reconnoitered fields in perfect rings. She was
barely grown before Major had bestowed upon her his highest
compliment: damn good dog.*

*But by the time dawn broke Monday morning, it seemed
Lady was a damn dead dog. She was gone, her pen was destroyed and her house had been sucked up into the tornado's
maw. Major's house was gone, too, with only a few bits of tim-
ber and siding left behind to suggest that a structure had once
occupied this spot. But a house and its contents can be re-
placed; a dog like Lady only comes along once.*

*Grief can play strange tricks on the mind. All morning long,
as he worked in the yard to salvage what he could from the
mess, Major heard Lady calling to him from the other side of
the great divide. In his mind, he heard her whimper her unhappiness from the heavens. After several hours of steady toil,
he stopped to rest, and it was then that a neighbor came over
to compare notes on damage. The neighbor was there only for
a few moments before he raised his eyes and squinted up into
the sun.*

*"Major," he finally said, "ain't you gonna get your dog
down from that tree?"*

Truth be told and prizes notwithstanding, it's not that I'm all
that good. It's just that most journalism isn't worth the paper
it's badly printed on.

Taken individually, reporters and editors tend to be bright,
charming people. When they gather in a crowd to produce a

newspaper, however, the result is usually horrid: a publication that manages to be both resolutely inoffensive and preachily purposeful. You'll die of boredom if you aren't driven off by the hectoring first. But then, most things done in groups end badly. If you need proof of that, attend a political convention. Or a war.

Of course, I knew none of this when I walked into the Barrington *Chronicle* in 1965 to ask for a job. I was twenty years old and full of pepper, ready for adventure of some kind. I'd given the military some thought and had even visited a few recruiters, but the results were inauspicious. The navy man gave me his best see-the-world pitch, but you had to sign on for four years and he couldn't talk around the fact that most of that time would be spent at sea exclusively in the company of men, although he went to great lengths to assure me all of them were thoroughly heterosexual.

"There's pussy in every port," he said. "I've had 'em all—Oriental, colored, Spanish. I prefer a Chinaman myself." He didn't seem to notice the slip.

The air force recruiter, after learning I had two years of college, appealed to my intellectual vanity: The air force required the highest test scores of any branch of the service, he said, painting it as the military equivalent of Mensa. Great, I thought. Four years with people who discuss thrust and lift, and not even be talking about getting laid.

I didn't bother with the marine corps recruiter. I was bored, not crazy.

It was the army recruiter, though, who put me off the military for good. "You ought to think about the Korean option," he said.

"What's that?" I asked.

"You do thirteen months in Korea after basic training, and we guarantee you spend the rest of your hitch anywhere you want in the free world."

"Including Australia?" This was promising. I'd had a long-distance enchantment with Australia for years, which was rooted in a television documentary I'd seen once that painted the country as a land of opportunity, filled with hail-fellow-well-met men and golden-skinned women who looked like California starlets but sounded (and hopefully fornicated) like Lady Caroline Lamb.

"Nah, anywhere except Australia."

"How 'bout South America?" Argentina was my emergency backup fantasy.

"We don't have bases in South America."

"Well, where do you have bases?"

"We're starting to send lots of people to Vietnam," he said hopefully.

I also briefly considered the Peace Corps, but two encounters with its officials caused me to realize that here was a mutant nightmare in the making: a federal bureaucracy infused with missionary zeal.

Finally, I decided to become a foreign correspondent. I wrote to the international editor of *The New York Times* and suggested that my complete lack of experience in journalism—coupled with my inability to speak any language but English and a travel background that consisted of a single bus trip to New York City and a summer of aimless hitchhiking—could give the *Times* a fresh perspective on foreign affairs that it likely wasn't getting from older, jaded hands. I said I would supply my own trench coat, but that the *Times* would need to give me the names and addresses of a few women of easy virtue in whatever city it sent me—Vienna or Paris would be acceptable—who might act as my pilot through the social strata. Oh, and salary is negotiable, I said, but I can't promise to be scrupulous about receipts for my expense account.

I got a bemused reply within a week. The editor said I had a remarkable and rare grasp of the life of a correspondent, and that copies of my letter of application had been forwarded to every international bureau with a note attached remarking that the next generation of reporters was showing promise, and that grizzled old fools who think they're secure in their posts should beware. He also suggested that I put in a few years at a newspaper somewhere else, because the *Times* was run by hidebound editors who demand experience; and that I get some practice at meeting women on my own, since the *Times*'s foreign desk leaves pimping and pandering to the Washington correspondents.

As it turned out, he remembered me years later when, after my self-loathing drew acclaim from all quarters, I had fled Barrington. He was the fool who hired me.

■

Taking the *Times* editor's advice, I presented myself at the Barrington *Chronicle*'s newsroom on a Monday morning to ask for the worst job available.

"Got lots of bad ones," the editor said. "Hard to say which is the worst. Probably headline writer."

"Why's that?" I asked.

"Because no matter what the story is, I always hate the headline. You'd think after twenty-eight years I'd have seen a headline I liked." He shook his head. "Hasn't happened yet."

Two desks away, a woman with a pencil was working her way through a stack of paper, scribbling marks and notes with an aggressive impatience. "He wouldn't know a good headline if it bit him on the butt," she said without looking up.

"Ignore her," the editor said. "She's still pissed off that God didn't give her the right equipment."

"You got the dick and I got the brain," she said. "So we're both well equipped to do our jobs." She transferred the last paper in front of her to one of the many untidy stacks on her desk, then stalked off.

The editor watched her go, then turned back to me and

shrugged. "I'd be unhappy, too, if I spent my life talking to Junior Leaguers. Why should I hire you?"

I knew he'd ask, but I still didn't have much of an answer. What was I supposed to say? I was a college dropout whose most notable achievement was a recent cross-continent hitchhiking odyssey, four months of near-constant movement interrupted only by a twenty-day sentence to a county work camp on a vagrancy charge in Montana. After the four students had dropped me off that spring day and continued on to Florida—continued on with lives that presumably were happy and orderly, spent among people like themselves—I realized I might find a perverse comfort in being completely and literally adrift in the world. I had returned to school, collected the few things I wanted to preserve—my driver's license, Social Security card, a pair of letters from Almo Hardy and a few photographs—and jammed them all into an empty coffee jar. After screwing the lid tight and melting candle wax around the lip to seal it, I buried it late at night in the yard outside my dormitory, one hand span away from the gnarled root that we had used as first base during intramural softball games. I left an hour later with $62 in my pocket, a change of clothes in a backpack and two letters in hand, one to the dean explaining that a family emergency would keep me out of class for a while and one to my mother telling her I'd be in touch. I dropped them into a mailbox at the edge of town.

I lived at the most basic level of barter. I learned there were a thousand minor chores to be done at any truck stop, and that if you checked in with the manager after arriving it would be only minutes before he pointed you out to a trucker who needed a hand shifting his load around or cleaning up his cab. They're a generous bunch, and even the simplest job was worth five bucks and a ride. Sometimes, they wanted nothing more than company as they drove, and I gave full value: I listened to them talk, asked questions about their lives and nodded in approval at all the right moments. I became an extractor of information, unknowingly training for my later life.

I wandered through twenty-seven states, and only at one point did anyone ask my name or even anything about me. The policeman who found me asleep in a riverside park in downtown Great Falls, Montana, snoozing peacefully no more than twenty steps from a sign prohibiting overnight camping, asked who I was. So did the booking officer at the jail, and so did the judge the next morning. I gave them all the same answer.

"Alexis de Tocqueville," I said, which became "Alex Tokebill" on the arrest report and subsequent court documents.

"Do you have some identification, Mr. Tokebill?" the judge asked. He was a stately old gentleman, hawk-nosed and lean, with a nice crop of white hair swept straight back. I'd noticed when he entered the courtroom that he wore cowboy boots and whipcord pants under his robe, making me wonder if there wasn't a ranch nearby that he'd prefer to be tending rather than sparring with uncooperative drifters.

"No, sir, I don't."

"Where are you from, Mr. Tokebill?"

"Pretty much all over," I said. He was silent for a moment, so I added: "Sir."

"Mr. Tokebill, the sign in the park couldn't be more clear. Why did you choose to sleep there?"

"Well, sir, when I stopped at the Cattleman's Hotel, they told me all the suites were taken," I said. The court clerk, sitting at a small table in front of the judge, stopped writing and looked up for the first time, while the bailiff beside me was suddenly alert.

The judge regarded me for a moment, then sighed. "Mr. Tokebill, what I usually do in a situation like this is ask the sheriff to simply give you a lift to the county line and send you on your way. But I believe, in this instance, you might be well served by cutting brush with a county work crew for ten days.

It might give you a little respect for the law and time to practice holding your tongue. Although I doubt it'll do much good."

"You're right, sir," I said.

"It'll do some good?" he asked, surprised.

"No, sir. You were right to doubt it."

"Let's make it twenty days," he said.

My companions on the work crew were wife beaters, drunks, petty thieves, brawlers, and a seventeen year old who had broken into his high school one night and dropped a turd on the principal's desk, inadvertently leaving his wallet as well. We worked all day, and they smoked cigarettes and talked in the dormitory at night about drinking and women. I realized pretty quickly that this was what the future held for the nameless and the rootless. I also realized that a disappearance, even a belated one, might possibly make my grandfather happy.

So when my twenty days were up, I headed home.

■

"Because I can talk to truck drivers," I said.

"Gee. And I just filled the long-distance-hauling beat," the editor said. "Do you speak French? I have an opening on the Paris fashion beat."

"I can talk to anybody."

"Yeah, but right now you're only talking to me, and we're not getting anywhere."

"Goddamn. It ain't for lack of trying," I said. "I'm playing my part. I'm the young pup who'll take the sorriest job you've got." The cause seemed to be lost, so I figured I may as well go down firing. "Did you forget your lines?"

But the editor just grinned. "Maybe I did. What are my lines?"

"'Sonny, I'll give you a week. You'd better show me something.'"

He nodded. "Sonny, I'll give you a week. You'd better show me something."

"Starting today?" I asked.

"Be back here at three. You'll do night cops. If you're lucky, somebody'll die."

I got lucky on my third night.

CHAPTER FOUR

*Just like there are no atheists in foxholes, there are no oppo-
nents to the proposed child-restraint law among cop reporters.*

*Surely you've heard of the proposed law. State Sen. Sallie
Snyder, who represents one of those northside Atlanta suburbs
filled with liberal handwringers, wants to make it a crime to
not buckle your child's seat belt while in a car. She says two recent car crashes in Atlanta—which together killed three un-
buckled children—prove that adults are careless. She says we
can't be trusted to look after our children. She says you're
damn right it's government intrusion, and if you don't like it,
tough. If you're alive when the next election rolls around, vote
against her.*

*As you might imagine, many people are unhappy with Sny-
der. Although we claim to like politicians who shoot straight,
it's alarming to encounter one who says she'll jam a law down
our throats simply because it's the right thing to do.*

*One of those unhappy people is Barrington's Charlie Har-
vey, who is head of the Soque County Taxpayers Action
Group.*

*Charlie came to see me Tuesday. He does that periodically.
Life is a continuing series of outrages against common, decent
people, and Charlie's mission in life apparently is to make sure*

I understand that most of those outrages can be traced back to government. No political action is innocent. In fact, in Charlie's world the most well-meaning proposals harbor—somehow, somewhere—the most sinister of purposes.

And Snyder's child-restraint bill is but the latest example.

"The simple act of getting in your car and driving to work shows how much we let government control every aspect of life," Harvey says. "The car is licensed by the government. The driver is licensed by the government. Speed limits are posted for every inch of road, and enforced by the government. You get your car inspected at facilities approved by the government. If the car doesn't meet standards mandated by the government, the facility reports you to the government."

(Author's note: He really talks this way, folks.)

"Do I think children should be buckled into their seats? Yes. [Vigorous nod of the head.] Do we need Mrs. Snyder ordering us to do it? No. [Emphatic shake of the head.] What's next? A law telling us which radio station to listen to as we drive?" (Long pause, which is my cue to pump my fist in the air and shout, "Damn right!")

Sorry, Charlie. You're damn wrong.

Instead of arguing with Charlie, I showed him a photograph. I had to root around in the clutter of my desktop before I found it: a stark black-and-white picture taken at night and lit only with a single flash. Darkness claims the edges of the photo, focusing your eyes on the image of two wrecked cars and, between them, a small body in the road with a sheet thrown over it.

I slid my chair over to Charlie's, and sat knee-to-knee while we looked at the picture. I told him the body was that of a four-year-old girl named Christine. I explained that her death was one of the first things I'd covered as a reporter, and that the memory of it was firmly fixed in my memory. Christine was riding with her mother on a rural highway, not buckled in but instead standing up in the front seat, when a drunk driver swerved into their lane. The mother instinctively yanked the steering wheel to the left just before the collision, which meant that when Christine catapulted through the front of the car, her head hit that strip of steel that separates the windshield from the passenger-side window.

The horror is found in the details. I showed Charlie where the steel was visibly dented from the force of 38 pounds of little girl hitting it at 60 miles an hour. And I made sure he noted the windshield, which thanks to safety glass was shattered but still in place. In its middle was a Christine-sized hole, complete with the clear outline of a leg. You know how cartoon characters leave a hole in their exact shape when they run through walls? Well, Christine did that as she spun sideways and exited through the windshield, the top of her skull already cleaved off by the window post.

To his credit, Charlie didn't falter. "That's unfortunate," he said after I'd finished my show-and-tell. "But you're confusing two unrelated things. I'm talking about Big Brother. You're talking about parental neglect."

He could see, however, that I wasn't buying what he was selling. He left a few minutes later. He was polite enough not to say what he doubtless felt: that I'm a sap who lets a single emotional memory cloud the big picture.

I'm polite, too, so I didn't say what we think. Me and Christine, that is.

I still have that photograph. The editor gave it to me at the end of my first week, after telling me I had the job permanently.

"Keep it on your desk," he said. "Whenever you think you're doing some good in this business, look at it."

I treated it as a joke. "Thanks," I snickered.

"I'm serious. At some point, you'll begin to believe you're making a difference in the world. But you know what? No matter what you do, kids are still going to die. People are still going to be venal and stupid and corrupt. We don't prevent it. We don't even really slow it down much."

He was quiet for a moment, then added: "You're pretty good at this. But do you know what happens to people like you?"

"No."

"They really mess up some day."

"What do you mean?" I asked.

"Three things are going to happen to you. You'll get praised. You'll get proud. And you'll get careless. That's when you'll mess up. I haven't saved a single one of you. It's as sure as the seasons."

As fate surely meant for me to do, I ignored him. He was right, of course, although he didn't have the order quite down. The carelessness came first.

■

He had a full name, which was printed in the paper every day, but he was never called anything but Cooley, which was his last name. He'd already been editor of the *Chronicle* for eleven years when I arrived in 1965, and would serve another twenty years before keeling over in the newsroom one day, dead almost before he hit the floor. The tributes to him were energetic, even fulsome. Had he been alive and the deceased someone else, he would have snorted in contempt. Actually, he did snort in contempt: He left behind his own obituary, which was printed only after a long argument with the publisher and only on the condition that it be accompanied with a note explaining that no disrespect was intended, and that in fact these were Cooley's own words. It said:

James Dalton Cooley, longtime editor of the Barrington Chronicle, *died Jan. 23 after suffering a stroke. He was 64 years old.*

Cooley joined the Chronicle *in 1939 as a copy assistant, a* job typically given then to young men who will work extraordinarily hard so that their elders could spend time drinking. In the course of time, Cooley worked as a sports reporter, police reporter, city hall reporter, copy editor, assistant city editor, city editor, editorial page editor and managing editor. He was named editor in 1954 after all qualified candidates declined the job and the Chronicle's owners turned to him in despair.

Cooley's stewardship of the newspaper was notable only for its lack of distinction. His sole memorable moment came during the great peach surplus of 1959, when he offered to let beleaguered growers trade peaches for the price of a subscription. Largely thanks to Time magazine—which wrote a three-paragraph article on the offer and featured a photograph of Cooley sitting atop a pile of peaches—the world's attention was drawn to Barrington for an instant. But the magazine eventually turned back to more substantial matters, and the Chronicle was left with several hundred bushels of rotting peaches in its lobby, which attracted a great swarm of flies.

On orders from the Chronicle's owners, the cost of removing the peaches was ultimately deducted from Cooley's salary, as was the price of the flyswatters issued to all employees.

Here are the basic details of Cooley's life: He was born in Buford, Georgia, on March 1, 1920. His parents were Lucius R. Cooley and Maylene Richards Cooley, both of whom are dead. His one sibling, an older brother named Vanton Cooley, also is dead. And now Cooley himself is dead, which means—considering that neither he nor his brother married or produced children—this part of the world is now Cooley-free.

Because he had no heirs, Cooley arranged for his entire estate to be left to a trust fund administered by the owners of the Dew Drop Inn in Barrington. Any patron of the Inn may order one drink a day and have its cost covered by Cooley's estate, until the estate's funds are exhausted.

Under the terms set out by the trust fund, however, drinkers *are limited in their choice of beverage. In fact, they have only this option: peach brandy.*

Actually, Cooley wrote much more. The full text of it was widely circulated in the newsroom, and even though I was gone by then, I read it later. It was the bleakest, most cold-blooded review of a career I've ever read. None of us arrive at the last quarter of our lives particularly happy with the way things have gone; how can you? Unless you've had some happy idiot like Dr. Pangloss trailing along in your wake reminding you that you live in the best of all possible worlds, you can't help but dwell on the disasters. Pain lasts, while happiness flees. It's as immutable as gravity. But few of us feel it necessary to sit down at the end and chronicle our failures. His was a record of bad decisions, missed opportunities and a complete inability to alleviate suffering in any meaningful way. He'd seen several generations of reporters come and go, and he'd been unable to steer a single one of them away from the abyss. They marched toward the bright light that someone had told them was truth and goodness and service, and they never examined the ground before them, even as it fell away. They also never noticed that the light became more diffuse as the years passed, until it was a bare wink, distant and unpredictable.

Cooley tried to tell me, and when I wouldn't listen, he wrote it down. I should have paid more attention.

■

Not long after I started work at the Barrington *Chronicle,* I visited my mother. I'd had no communication with her since posting the letter the night I left the university nearly two years before. Part of me reveled in knowing that my settlement a scant fifty miles from Doralee, and the appearance of my byline in the paper, meant word surely had trickled back that I had returned. For a while, it seemed perfect: I was far enough away to be out of my grandfather's orbit, but close enough so that my silence was a message unto itself.

But guilt caught up. My mother was self-pitying and helpless, and had worked ceaselessly to make victimhood her defining characteristic. But a son should not be another torment.

I set out at midmorning one Sunday, calculating my time so that I would be sitting on the porch when they returned from church. It was my way of sidestepping the question of whether I was now required to knock. Rapping on the door of the home I'd grown up in would seem like a victory for my grandfather. But throwing it open and walking in would rob me of the opportunity to make clear my own sense of separation. Besides, the old bastard might have shot me and later claimed he thought I was an intruder.

It didn't matter, as it turned out. I arrived in Doralee earlier than I expected, and stopped by Almo Hardy's store to kill a few minutes. He told me.

"You been in touch with your mother?" he asked. His tone was precisely, carefully neutral.

I suddenly felt rotten. "Well, not as often as I should," I lied. "But I talked to her the other day."

"No, you didn't," he said.

I didn't reply, and for a moment we just stared at each other.

"She ain't doing much talking these days," he finally said. "Or let me put it this way: She may be talking, but she ain't having conversations."

"What do you mean?"

"You haven't heard any of this, have you?"

"Any of what?"

"Oh, Jesus," he said.

"What?" I said again.

"Your mother got sent to Milledgeville."

It was my turn to say it. "Oh, Jesus."

Anyone who grew up in Georgia would understand the reference. Milledgeville is a small city where the state's mental hospital is located. Over time, its very name had become a code word for the drastic treatment imposed on the truly demented: those who wander the streets babbling, commune with aliens, carry on long conversations with Jesus while sitting on bus benches or suggest out loud that Negroes are just people, too, so why not marry them? To say someone needed to be sent to Milledgeville was to say their lunacy was permanent and deep. And it wasn't a place where you were turned over to the care of a friendly Jungian therapist whose forehead would crinkle with concern as you poured out your troubles as the two of you strolled about the manicured lawn. It was instead—at least at the time—the place where your dosage or voltage was increased until you and Jesus stopped having your heart-to-heart talks.

"What happened?" I said.

"Nobody knows exactly, except your grandfather. And the judge who signed the commitment order, I guess. Collie's always stayed pretty close to home, as you know. I wouldn't see her for weeks at a time, and even then she'd only come down here for cigarettes when she was desperate."

I'd spent enough time in Almo's store to doubt his proclamation of ignorance. For years, I'd hovered on the fringes of countless clusters of men as they dawdled by the cash register to talk. I knew that in a town where even a sudden cold front could keep talk alive for days, my mother's institutionalization would have been a hot topic for weeks.

"What happened?" I asked again.

"Well, I did hear some things. But people talk, you know. You never know what to believe."

Almo was clearly uncomfortable. His hands were jammed into his pockets, and his gaze kept shifting to the window, as if he hoped to draw a customer in through force of will and derail our conversation.

"Hear what things?"

"Apparently she kept talking about someone taking her baby. She started calling the sheriff's office every day to say her baby was gone. Then she began calling around to other places. People say she was even pestering the governor's office."

"What baby? Does anybody know what she's talking about?"

"I don't think so. Your grandfather had the phone cut off for a while, but then she started writing letters." His eyes went to the window again. "She mailed one here."

"What did it say?"

"It said a monster came into her room one night and snatched a baby from her arms. Her baby."

"Oh, Jesus." I sat on a milk crate and leaned my back against the upright cooler. "Is that all?"

"Sounded like enough for the judge, I guess," Almo said, turning back to face me. "Look, no one blames your grandfather. He put up with it for a long time. But eventually he had to do something, you know?"

■

I decided to knock, but as I drove up the road I saw it was unnecessary. My grandfather was sitting on the porch.

He watched me carefully as I parked and got out of the car. Like Almo, he was unsure how much I knew, so he waited for me to speak first. I climbed the steps and sat on the porch swing. The creaking of its chains was the only sound for a few moments, until I asked, "So how is she?"

"She's better," he said.

"Is she here?"

"Inside watching television. Go in if you want." He seemed almost cordial.

"How long was she there?"

"About a month or so. They said she responded to her treatment quite nicely."

"What kind of treatment was it?"

"I'm not sure, exactly. A doctor explained it to me when I visited one time. But he seemed like a nice fella, and he said she'd be fine."

"So you just packed her off to the lunatic asylum and let some witch doctor do whatever he wanted."

His cordiality vanished. "So where were you? You just drop out of sight for so long, she thinks you're dead. Then that becomes a baby being taken from her at night. Then she starts hiding from me and whispering into the telephone, and then the sheriff stops in one day to ask me all kinds of strange questions. So I've got to wrestle with all that, and now that the dirty work's been done, you pop up. Sit on my porch, on my swing"—he came down hard on the "my" both times—"and make it sound like I've done something wrong."

"Sorry," I muttered.

I stood and went inside. I found her in the back of the house, sitting by a window in the sunlight. Her clothes were new and stylish, and her hair was brushed and pinned away from her face. She looked better than I remembered her.

She turned toward the door and smiled when I came in. "Oh, there you are, sweetie," she said. "Did you see your grandfather out there? We need to be thinking about lunch."

■

My blindness probably took root that day. She was happy and unburdened, humming as she set out lunch and smiling to herself. My grandfather's flash of anger had passed and he seemed to be trying to soothe things with me, citing the few lukewarm memories we shared and relating gossip from around town. We all had a cup of coffee after lunch, then another. Milledgeville was not mentioned.

For my part, I recounted my adventures of the past two

years, turning my hitchhiking odyssey into a romp around the countryside and making the county work camp sound like a summer job. I also caught up on the things that had been in flux when I'd left. After being busted down from his foreman's job at the mill, my grandfather had decided his ambition had been misplaced, anyway; he was happy not to have to worry about other workers, content instead to tend to his own machine.

"Besides, rumor is they're going to lay off some managers," he said. "It's best to be doing real work when jobs start disappearing."

That nudged my memory elsewhere. "Speaking of disappearing, did Jack ever turn up?" Jack had been my childhood dog, a forlorn pup I'd found in the ditch while on my way to Almo's one day and had been allowed to keep against all expectations. He'd stayed with us for ten years, until the day he strayed from sight shortly after I'd departed for college. That happens in the country. Dogs lose arguments with cars and die quietly in roadside ditches.

"I never found him," my grandfather said. "But I didn't have much time to look. That was when things were, ah . . . getting unsettled around here." My mother, busy at the sink, didn't seem to hear, and I was touched by my grandfather's delicacy. He clearly saw no benefit to dwelling on the recent unhappiness.

After a couple of hours, I helped clear the table, kissed my mother on the cheek, shook my grandfather's hand and waved good-bye as I drove away, leaving them standing on the porch together. My mind sifted through the evidence as I headed for Barrington, and I finally concluded that things can change: Mothers can get better, grandfathers can become benevolent and whole episodes of childhood can be placed in the category of imagined memories. In a burst of resolve, I decided I would change, too. I would write and occasionally visit. I would be less quick to judge. I would offer the benefit of the doubt. And I would do this in all parts of my life.

The erosion of that resolve was long and subtle, spread over several years. By the time the woman from the trailer court called, it was gone.

CHAPTER FIVE

Like so many other things in life, the whole dispute isn't really about what the two men say it's about.

The two men are neighbors, occupants of adjoining homes located on Barrington's near east side. They have lived next door to each other for 15 years. Their names are Preston Hendrix and Joe Salvi.

Even before the dispute, the men weren't buddies. Sure, they waved to one another and occasionally chatted in the yard. But they don't have much in common. They have different friends. They have different hobbies. They have different tastes in television shows. They have different political leanings.

They also have different kinds of jobs: Salvi wears a tie, while Hendrix works with his hands.

After Salvi puts on his tie every morning, he drives to an office and does his work there. After Hendrix puts on his coveralls every morning, he walks to his garage and does his work there. And that's where the problem lies. Salvi wants the Barrington Zoning Board of Appeals to tell Hendrix to do his work somewhere else.

Hendrix fixes cars. On any given day, he repairs one car while another three or four are parked on the street awaiting their turns. There's an almost constant shuffling of cars in and out of the Hendrix garage, as well as the usual noise of a repair facility: engines racing, dropped tools ringing off the concrete, air wrenches screaming against lug nuts, and a radio tuned to country music turned up loud. Hendrix tends to sing along, Salvi says. "He thinks he's some kind of Merle Haggard or something."

Salvi says he paid good money for a nice home in a quiet neighborhood. He says Barrington's zoning regulations clearly prohibit commercial enterprises in residential areas. He says he asked Hendrix to consider moving his business to another location, and even scouted a few possible sites for him in a friendly, neighborly sort of way. He says Hendrix pretended to consider moving, but finally admitted that he didn't want to pay rent, didn't want to fool with getting a city business license and didn't see why he couldn't just stay right where he was.

So Salvi has asked the zoning board to tell Hendrix to work somewhere else.

The matter came up at the zoning board's meeting Tuesday night. Because the board is a model of single-mindedness, and because it prefers not to referee all sorts of side issues, it usually focuses on a single question: Is the zoning code being violated?

In this case, the simple answer is yes. So Hendrix was doomed when the board chairman—who, like the rest of us, prefers a simple answer—asked if cars were being repaired in the garage and is this your primary income, just say yes or no, please.

But life usually is more complicated than yes or no.

It turns out that Hendrix has provided free repairs to Salvi's cars for years. Hendrix knew his work was sometimes noisy, so it seemed like a way to make up for it. For a long time this was a workable arrangement between neighbors, right up until the day the air-conditioning compressor on Salvi's car went out.

"The stuff I'd done for him before didn't cost me much. Tune-ups, oil and lube, a rebuilt alternator once, stuff like that," Hendrix says. "But one day, he comes home from work and pulls straight into my driveway. He's all sweaty, with his tie loose, and he says, 'Hey, you gotta fix my air-conditioning.'

"Now that bothered me a little, 'cause it sounded like an order. You know, like he's my boss or something. But I tell him to pull his car into the garage, and after I pop the hood on it I can see it's probably the compressor. So I tell him that, and then I tell him they're expensive, could be a couple of hundred bucks. He just looks at me for a second, then says, 'Yeah, so?'"

The conversation apparently deteriorated from that point. Hendrix says Salvi told him he wanted the air-conditioning fixed for free, or he would complain to the city about the operation of an unlicensed garage. Hendrix says his response was to offer to give the defective compressor a permanent home in Salvi's bowels. The two men haven't talked since.

For his part, Salvi won't say much about the compressor, except to deny that his complaint to the zoning board was related to it. When asked about the details of the matter—the years of free car service, for instance, and the fact that his complaint was filed only days after the argument over the compressor—he just shrugs.

"None of that matters," he says. "I'm just looking out for the neighborhood."

The zoning board also is looking out for the neighborhood. It ordered Hendrix to close his car-repair shop next week. He's visited numerous garages looking for work, but nothing has turned up. He's afraid he may have to apply for food stamps.

For his part, Salvi appreciates the quiet—so much so, in fact, that he's planning to quit his job and turn a spare bedroom into a home office. He's going to be a consultant now.

He says he's already checked with the zoning board. A home office is just fine.

By the time the woman in the trailer park called, I had covered 229 zoning board meetings, 358 city council meetings, 192 county commission meetings and an even dozen sewer board meetings. I had thumbed through eleven thousand police reports, scanned fifty thousand names entered into the Soque County jail log and attended hundreds of trials, sentencings and arraignments. I had visited the scene of countless car accidents, house fires, chemical spills, train derailments, murders, robberies and natural disasters. I had seen my fellow humans at their most pitiful, most bureaucratic and most callous. Occasionally I saw dignity or courage—witnessed the stirring of some noble instinct—but not often. It rarely happens, you know. Life offers us only a few opportunities to act wisely and bravely, and when it does we'll usually make a hash of it. Guaranteed.

At first, I embraced my assignments with a missionary's vigor. Each day brought a new twist on the human condition and each interview was a test of my ability to discern it. I was not just a reporter and the Barrington *Chronicle* was not just a newspaper; I was instead the speaker in an ancient Greek drama, and the *Chronicle* was my chorus.

"Sometimes a cat stuck in a tree is just a cat stuck in a tree," Cooley said one day. "Not everything is high drama."

This was a conversation we'd had before: Cooley counseling me to take the measure of events and parcel my labor accordingly, me responding that every tale is worth telling well.

"I don't want to bore readers," I said.

"I'm not worried about readers," he said. "I'm worried about you."

"Why?"

"Because you'll lose your taste for it. Then when a real drama presents itself someday, it'll seem like just another cat stuck in a tree."

Indeed, things began to repeat themselves over the years, taking on a deadening predictability: I heard the same political issues argued, saw the same petty crimes committed by the powerful, listened to the same piteous complaints from the oppressed. And I wearied of it.

∎

My mother also had begun to repeat herself.

Her peculiar madness was not to be denied. Stealthy and relentless, it stalked her for years, claiming bits of buried memory and assembling them into familiar, horrible shapes in a dark corner away from her consciousness. Then at random moments, it would flash a picture into her mind and let it linger for a single terrifying second.

A pattern established itself. After several viewings, she would become withdrawn and sullen, avoiding my grandfather and hiding whenever the rare visitor arrived. Later, she would seek to share the details of some purported horror she'd suffered, scratching out notes on paper ripped from grocery bags and leaving them in the mailbox for the postman to find, or whispering into the phone to puzzled secretaries at countless government offices. Eventually my grandfather would obtain another court order and my mother would be strapped down for another few jolts of juice. Then she would be docile and lucid for a while.

But that was also when she was at her most helpless. In the grip of her madness, she at least sought to do something, spinning out her fantastic tales and demanding justice. In her calm, she did little but wring her hands.

"I wish things were different," she said one day. I was making one of my periodic visits during the long, uncertain peace with my grandfather, and this was the start of a common conversation between us.

"Different how?" I asked.

"I wish I wasn't Collie anymore." *Anymoah.* I was my father hearing her voice for the first time, drawn by the sound but not the words.

"I think Collie's just fine," I said.

"No, she isn't. I'm a mess, honey. I hate living here with him, but I can't leave." *Heah. Cain't.*

"Sure you can. You just go. This is America. You won't go hungry."

"You make it sound so easy," she said. "I suppose it is easy for men. You can just wander off for a year and be no worse for it." This was the second half of her lament: I'd left her alone.

"I've never understood what's so awful about it," I said. "Maybe he's not the friendliest guy in the world, but at least he looks after you during your bad spells."

"He is my bad spell."

"No, he's not. He's just like anyone else. He's just trying to make it to the end of the day."

My grandfather had benefited from the passage of time. Every day at work, as I recorded a bit more of the world's malice and treachery, his image softened with each word. I had concluded he was an amateur at torment; his heart wasn't in it. He may have loomed large over my childhood, a menacing and malignant presence, but he now seemed just peculiar and pitiful. Age had made him small, and whatever power of intimidation he'd had was long gone. I sometimes wondered how I'd had the energy to hate him so vigorously for so long.

Besides, he'd made me a co-conspirator in my mother's treatment. When her madness hinted at its desire to return at some point after the first cure, he'd made his only visit to me in Barrington. We had coffee in my regular restaurant, where he sat, contrite and vulnerable, and allowed me to see him as someone who sincerely regretted some of his choices in life. There are things a man just does, he said, and one of them is to bull your way through adversity. Life had taken his wife early and left him with a peculiar daughter, and that daughter had behaved recklessly, embarrassing him and herself. To meet this circumstance with anything but anger—anything but a cold, hard refusal to accept it—at the time had seemed like weakness, he said. But he now saw that was wrong, he said.

I learned much about him that afternoon, a day in which he

addressed me by name and introduced himself proudly as my grandfather when the waitress refilled our cups and offered me my usual dose of good-natured abuse. I never knew he'd played baseball well enough to have once been invited to a professional team tryout. I never heard he'd danced well enough to be considered a catch by girls in three counties, and had owned one of the first cars in the area, which gave him the chance to plumb those affections. I listened as he talked about his own stern grandfather, the one-armed, hook-nosed old rogue who had fought in the war of secession and filled his grandson's head with glorious tales of battle, imbuing him with a warrior's toughness and a loser's alienation.

It was clear my grandfather had launched into his life with confidence and spirit, only to find himself years later wondering how to confront the madness of a daughter who whispered horrible things to strangers. He asked for my help.

The pattern of my life is consistent: I've always said yes at the wrong moments. When the next request for involuntary treatment was filed with the court, it carried both our signatures.

■

"You just don't understand," she said.

We sat on the porch without speaking for long minutes as the twilight came, me on the step with my back against the railing, my mother in the swing pushing herself with a toe, causing the chain to groan rhythmically where it was hooked into the ceiling. In the yard, the fireflies winked their message in a slow-motion Morse code.

I finally broke the silence. "Well, what would you like to do?"

"There's nothing to be done," she said. As always, helplessness triumphed.

■

The call came in the morning.

"Tad Beckman," I said into the phone.

"Is this Tad Beckman?" a woman's voice said.

"Yes," I said. Great. More evidence of the high-caliber intellect of my readership.

She wasn't satisfied. "Tad Beckman, who writes that column?"

"Yes," I said again, drawing it out with a menacing patience.

"I didn't think I'd get to talk to you."

I didn't respond. I had neither time nor patience for this. After a moment, she said, "Are you still there?"

"I'm right here, ma'am. Is there something you wanted to tell me?"

"You don't sound like I expected you to sound."

Again, I said nothing. I shifted back in my seat and propped a leg up on the edge of the desk. It was still early in the newsroom, but the few people who had arrived for work lifted their heads my way and I sensed their expectant grins. I had a reputation for not suffering fools gracefully, and my phone conversations were a source of common amusement.

"You there?" she said again.

"Yes, ma'am."

"Well, the thing I wanted to know is, how do you write columns?"

"How do I write columns?" I repeated. I sometimes did that for the benefit of my newsroom audience.

"Yeah. I mean, how do you decide what to write about?"

"Is there a reason why you're asking me these questions?"

"Well, sort of. I know about something you could maybe write about."

"Oh?" I said, making it sound both challenging and doubtful.

It was her turn to be silent for a moment. Finally, she said, "I thought you'd be nicer."

"You thought I'd be nicer?" I again echoed. I heard a snicker from a nearby desk.

"I hoped you might be able to help me. Isn't that what you do? Help people?"

Her voice was brittle and I suddenly realized she was near hysteria.

"What do you need help with?" I asked, softening my tone.

It was too late. She'd already started crying. "No one will help me. He's gonna kill me someday and nobody's doing a thing about it."

I gritted my teeth in frustration. I knew I was going to get mired in this phone call. My early warning system had told me right away that this was trouble, but here I was. Calls such as this one come to newspapers daily, and reporters either quickly learn to avoid such encounters or they spend great chunks of their lives paddling fruitlessly in the endless ocean of other people's self-pity. It's the great unacknowledged credo of newspapering: We're here to help, unless you ask for it.

But I had let her start, now decency demanded I hang on for the duration.

"Who's going to kill you, ma'am?" I asked.

"My ex-husband. I've told the police this, but they won't do anything."

"You filed a complaint and they won't act on it?"

"Well, not exactly."

"What do you mean, then?"

"I know he's gonna hurt me. I can tell, but no one will listen to me."

"Has he hurt you before?" I was standing by then, stretching all the coils out of the phone cord as I tried unsuccessfully to reach the coffeepot. I waved my cup hopefully in the direction of my fellow reporters, but they just smirked; it wasn't until I caught the summer intern's eye and glowered that it got filled. When I sat down again, I reached for the sports section.

"He's wanted to."

"But he hasn't."

"Not yet," she said.

"What did the police say?"

"They said they can't arrest people for crimes they haven't committed yet."

"That's generally true," I said.

"A lot of good that does me."

"Ma'am, I'm still not sure I understand what's going on." Even as I said it, I knew it was a mistake.

"Well, I'll tell you," she said. I slapped my head in frustration.

It was an ordinary white-trash drama, told in an annoyingly ragged and disorganized fashion. She lived in a trailer park on one of Barrington's poorer edges, a place that rookie police dispatchers learn about on their first weekend at work. She'd married young, but things had gone sour after a few years. He drank, lost jobs and threw meals against the wall. She scrounged food stamps, cleaned up his messes and tried to make the children understand that his behavior wasn't their fault. Eventually, they divorced.

But that hadn't been the end of it. He'd asked to come back, and when she refused him, he'd begun harassing her: phone calls at all hours, dead wildlife left by the trailer's door, unsigned letters that vaguely hinted at retribution for imagined sins.

"And he's always around," she said. "If I go to the grocery store, he'll get in line behind me and not say anything. Or I'll see his car parked at the end of the road, sort of pulled behind a tree like he's trying to hide it, but you can tell he really wants me to see it. And he's all the time coming to the plant where I work, watching me leave in the afternoon to see who I'm talking to."

"You told all this to the police?"

"Yes. They said it ain't against the law to watch somebody."

I sighed. Nothing ever came of these tales. I was supposed to craft a column out of an ex-husband's weird behavior? Who cares? I'd heard all this a hundred times before. I was tired of this conversation well before the phone rang. "I don't think I can help you with this," I said.

"Why not?" she asked. In the background a television was turned on and off abruptly, and I imagined a small child wandering just beyond her reach.

"I'm not sure what I can do. I can't make him stop bothering you."

"Maybe you could get the police to make him stop."

"I don't have as much influence as you think I do."

"I've seen what you write. You could embarrass them."

"You want me to humiliate the people you might need someday?"

"I don't know what else to do."

Suddenly I was talking to my mother. "You could move away. Just leave. Put the kids in the car, go to the grocery store and simply don't come back." I heard my own voice rising. "Don't wait around for other people to solve this for you. You can't wish things away. I'm sorry this has happened, but I can't fix it for you."

I heard her crying again, which made me even angrier. "Just go away," I said.

I meant that she should move away. But she took me at my word. She hung up.

■

A week later, Cooley appeared at my elbow. It was late afternoon and the production shift had already settled in, readying themselves for their nightly chore of measuring copy, cropping photographs, writing headlines and generally laboring earnestly to produce a newspaper that will be either ignored or reviled the next morning. I was pretending to study some government documents, waiting for enough time to pass so that my exit wouldn't seem indecently early.

"Something just came across on the police radio," Cooley said. "You might be interested."

The cat had climbed the tree.

CHAPTER SIX

The four-year-old boy walked out into the glare of spotlights Thursday night and, in that matter-of-fact way small children have, told police what the problem was inside the mobile home:

"Mommy's head came off."

The commander wanted to know more, but he was waved away by a matronly neighbor, who enveloped the boy in one great arm and led him into the darkness, where she could try to whisper his nightmare away. The frustrated commander turned his attention back to the home's door and resumed the vigil.

Soon, the other two children emerged. They were older, and the expressions on their faces made clear that they were beyond the ministrations of a kindly neighbor. The commander didn't even try to approach them; they, too, were hurried off into the darkness.

A while later, the object of everyone's attention also came out the door. He blinked rapidly several times, confused by the bright lights and apparently unable to see beyond them. He staggered a bit, perhaps drunk but maybe just tired. It had been, after all, a long night. In his right hand was a gun, which he held near his leg as he looked around. In his left hand was proof that the youngest child had correctly analyzed Mommy's problem.

When the commander called out, the man looked in the direction of the voice. Then, before he'd barely gotten his gun arm raised in front of him, he was killed.

She hadn't asked for much, really.

She'd called one day with a problem. People do that a lot. A few times in my life, I've been able to fix something. It's almost always been a small problem that likely would have worked itself out without me, but I stepped in and wrote about it, and then it got fixed. As a result, people think I have magical powers: They believe I can change things by writing about them.

The reality is much different. I can temporarily embarrass a public official, or I can make fun of a cumbersome bureaucratic process. I can make you feel sympathy for someone who got a raw deal. I can point out the obvious and make it seem clever. But I can't fix things.

She thought I could, however, so she called to tell me her problem. She'd been married for years to a drunken lout, a man who neglected his wife and children when he wasn't abusing them. For a long time, she believed love would cure him; then for another long time, she tried just staying out of his way. Finally, she divorced him and tried to get on with her life. She lived poor and worried about her children. But that wasn't her problem.

Her problem was that her ex-husband missed family life.

He hated the idea of having to work and stay sober. He hated not having someone else to blame for things. He missed the sweet feel of his hand smacking her face. Oh, how he wanted the comforts of home.

He asked to come back, and when she refused he began a campaign of terror and intimidation. Yet few of the things he did were overtly criminal, and those that were happened out of sight of any witness. So the police offered little beyond sympathetic noises and comforting clucks of the tongue. That's when she called me.

I didn't even offer that much.

She annoyed me. She seemed whiny and helpless, which is a combination I detest. I want my readers to be brave, noble and dignified. I want them to face adversity quietly. I want them to be available when I call, answer questions truthfully, speak in complete sentences and with earthy insight, then leave me alone. I want to marvel at quiet strength, not wring my hands with pity.

So I brushed her off. I had no desire to get mixed up in some trailer-park melodrama. I didn't think about her again until her ex-husband came out of the mobile home, carrying her severed head by the hair.

People keep telling me it wasn't my fault.

I know that's strictly true. The blame game has already begun, as you'll see on the front page of this newspaper today, and it doesn't involve me. Police logs have been reviewed and they show that the woman had called three times for help, each time explaining in explicit detail why she feared her ex-husband. Each time, the police looked hard at the law and found, regrettably, that they could do nothing. It's bunk, of course, a time-honored dodge among cops: You cite the law as a hindrance when you've got better things to do.

But I still feel guilty. Newspapers are supposed to be a kind of court of appeals. They are the place you visit when society's official instruments of justice have failed you. Yet when she asked to file her appeal of the death sentence, the court clerk was bored, cynical and disinterested.

As a result, the appeal was never heard. And the condemned was executed on schedule, just as she predicted.

I'm sorry. I wish I had a second chance.

Most thoughtful cultures have found their own way to say it, but the Roman statesman Seneca put it most succinctly: "Do not ask for what you will wish you had not got."

CHAPTER SEVEN

Some tenderhearted fool nominated me for a Pulitzer prize.

It wasn't Cooley. When, after the announcement was made, I asked him about it, he'd just snorted. He'd already told me he thought my confessional was the worst sort of grandstanding self-flagellation.

"What are you going to do when somebody calls and says he'll kill himself if we don't run 'Little Orphan Annie'?" he said.

"I'll transfer the call to you."

"That's a death sentence, then," he said. "I hate that goggle-eyed tramp. So you'd better go ahead and get started."

"Started on what?" I asked, walking right into it.

"Your next column. You know, the one lamenting that you transferred a call and someone died as a result."

I felt my face flush. "You're really a prick, you know."

"Yeah, probably," he said cheerfully. "But at least I'm con-sistent. You can't decide whether you want to be a tough guy or a tragic figure."

So it wasn't Cooley. And it wasn't the *Chronicle*'s publisher, a dapper old gent who was legendary in the newsroom for both his utter incomprehension of news events and his ability to nonetheless register grave looks of concern during his occa-sional appearances at the daily page-one meeting, where the

day's offering of tragic deaths, natural disasters, political blun-
derings and international tensions were weighed and measured.
He made his legend one morning with two simple questions.

"Who's Lech Walesa?" he asked. When the answer came, he
nodded thoughtfully, then posed his follow-up query.

"Where's Poland, exactly?"

So it had to be a reader. The Pulitzer committee accepts
nominations from anyone willing to fill out a form, photocopy
a few articles and write a nominating letter, and someone had
done just that. The committee—proving that journalism can
forgive anything provided it's written well—then awarded me
the prize.

Once I determined that no one at the *Chronicle* had made
the nomination, I stopped trying to find out who had. I suppose
the committee would have told me if I'd asked, but I didn't
want to know. What was I supposed to do? Call and thank him
for turning an act of contrition into a moment of glory? I could
hear myself: "Hello, this is Tad Beckman. Listen, it was pretty
obvious I felt bad about that lady, you know, with her getting
her head chopped off and all, but thanks to you, now I see it
was a good thing. Like they say, clouds and silver linings. How
'bout those kids, though? [Rueful chuckle here.] Hope they
shake it off. Why don't you nominate them for something?"

I left the *Chronicle,* and Barrington itself, a week later. When
Cooley came in the next morning, my desktop was completely
clear, except for the prize certificate placed in the middle with
the words "I quit" scrawled across it.

I headed for Florida, wasting a year in Key West before finally landing in Miami. It was there that I learned one reader
agreed with me: Glory, however unsolicited it may have been,
was not to be tolerated.

■

Actually, I meant to settle in Key West. History had always been a little too vivid for my taste—it was always something I was never part of but lived with nonetheless, an arranged marriage with an insistent but unlikeable partner who burrowed into my bed and being every day. So there was much appeal in a place where history didn't count for much. I thought of Key West as a place where the world's fringe dwellers lived together in the present, each of them uninterested in what had brought the others there and unconcerned with what would happen tomorrow. I, also, wanted to live only in the present.

I made the long drive down U.S. 1, hopscotching from key to key, on the first day of hurricane season, when saner creatures had already headed north, leaving the city to its natives and settlers. I took the cheapest lodgings I could find, a permanently damp room in a cinder-block motel on the eastern edge of the key, where the ticky-tacky sprawl greets visitors as they cross over from Stock Island and prompts them to wonder if the island's alleged charm and ambiance weren't in fact some grotesque joke.

The motel's other residents were members of the permanent underclass, and I soon joined them. I took a job pouring drinks at a bar off Duval Street. After a month of carefully saving my tips and living off bar snacks, I could afford to leave the motel for a room just three blocks from the bar, located in a decaying, gingerbread-laden old wreck of a home that looked like a Charles Addams cartoon sprung to life. The landlady was a Conch widow named Mrs. Reynolds, who set out the rules right away.

"I take cash only, every Monday," she said. "And I tolerate no buggery here. What you do is your own business, so long as you do it somewhere else."

She was loathed by her homosexual neighbors. They hoped to cash in on Key West's growth and had launched pricey renovations of their homes, but complained it was all for naught every time a prospective buyer passed the Reynolds manse, squatted in the middle of the block like a turd in a flower bed. Worse yet, the old girl had a taste for rum, and under its influence she sometimes stood on the porch and at the top of her voice shared her feelings about the neighborhood's changing character.

"Hey, sweet things," she called to a pair of male visitors one afternoon as they left the house next door after a tour with a real estate broker. "Did they give you the bad news? There's a woman next door." Then she made smooching noises and gave a fan dancer's wiggle, sending the men hurrying for their car.

Despite her homophobia, I liked her. She was a soft touch, it turned out, and most of her tenants were hopelessly in arrears, meaning the house—despite her seeming embrace of its decay—was actually a casualty of economics. It had been built by her grandfather, one of the island's original wreckers, and after she'd satisfied herself that I wasn't queer and therefore available to be looked in the eye safely without fear of having a perverse image flash into her mind, she began to tell me stories of her youth. Her history of the keys was both more interesting and much less benign than the chamber of commerce version. She told me the wreckers, far from being a happy bunch of beachcombers, were in fact a ruthless group who weren't above leaving the crew of a crippled ship to drown in a storm if the vessel's captain didn't agree to their salvage demands and that they ensured business remained steady by occasionally extinguishing the island's light on stormy nights, robbing ships of their bearings in the keys' treacherous waters. As she told these tales I could hear in her accent the half-dozen cultures that mingle in Key West, mixed together in an odd stew that simmers constantly in the tropical heat.

We became Saturday night pals. At the bar where I worked, Mrs. Reynolds would settle onto the single stool at the short leg of the L-shaped bar, next to the spot where the waitresses picked up their drink orders, and let me pour her a shot of rum every forty-five minutes or so. She would sit there for several hours until her own private closing bell rang, then seek to settle her tab by pulling crumpled one-dollar bills from random pockets in her clothes and piling them up on the bar. I always refused her money, so she tipped lavishly, leaving the pile, which I later converted to larger denominations and returned to her as payment for anything I may have claimed from her refrigerator.

We spent those nights talking. The conversations had an uncertain, erratic quality to them, with questions posed and then left unanswered for minutes at a time as I tended to patrons at the far end of the bar or hurried to fill the waitresses' orders as they stood three deep at Mrs. Reynolds's elbow. But she always kept track of the talk, and bore in when she sensed evasiveness.

"So what are you doing here?" she asked one night.

"Baby-sitting drunks," I said. "Somebody's got to do it."

"Not here, stupid. Here," she said, sweeping her arm in a wide arc to indicate the town outside.

I shrugged. "Just enjoying myself."

"It doesn't look like you're actually enjoying much."

"Oh?"

"In fact, you're pretty goddamn grim."

"Exactly how do people act when they're enjoying themselves?" I asked.

"Well, they don't act like you."

"What are they like, then?"

She hesitated as one of the waitresses rapped on the bar, demanding my attention and letting me know with a look that if she got stiffed on a tip, she preferred it be because she spilled a drink on a mainlander who had patted her fanny and not because some slackass barkeep was wasting time with an old Conch widow. Like most corners of paradise—like Aspen, like Jackson Hole, like Carmel—Key West had cleaved along an economic fault line, making residency a high-priced privilege and leaving its inhabitants conscious of every dollar.

"I guess I'm not sure," Mrs. Reynolds finally said when the waitress left. "But happy people don't act like they're in training."

■

It indeed seemed like training.

In the mornings I skipped rope two thousand times, breaking it down into four sets of five hundred and giving myself a fifteen-second rest between each set. An elaborate set of rules evolved over time: I had to add ten skips the first time I stepped on the rope and twenty-five every time after that; I had to spend the last fifty skips of each set hopping on one foot or the other; and I had to cross my hands on every other downward arc during the last set, a tricky maneuver that boxers perform effortlessly but always caused me to pile up the penalty skips.

Afterward, I would hook my toes under the railing on Mrs. Reynolds's porch and do a hundred slow sit-ups, then roll over and do fifty equally slow push-ups, dripping sweat from my nose onto the floorboards. Then I would walk for an hour, exploring Key West's narrow streets and forgotten neighborhoods before the heat became a bully. Only then would I eat and, if the night before had been late, sleep again for a while.

That is what I did. I had become like my mother, you see. Images would flash into my mind at random moments, graphic pictures of the man carrying his prize, showing the world he'd won. But I found that the twin metronomes, the skip of the rope and the push of my blood, helped keep the images at bay. That was the difference: She watched, I didn't.

Besides, my own flight had disgusted me. At the time, my departure had felt ennobling, the appropriate response to an undeserved moment of glory. After all, what fool walks away from a career-making honor? Only that one who feels profoundly regretful. Or so I told myself.

But after a few months in Key West I weighed that gesture on a different scale. I began to wonder precisely what was being accomplished in exile, privately debated whether living exclusively in the present really helped you hide from history or somehow perversely emphasized it, sort of like the crazed relative in the attic that no one acknowledges but no one can forget either. I also began to see that there was no penance involved.

I had not fled Barrington to labor selflessly in a poverty-stricken nation, for instance, or in a Calcutta slum or in some misbegotten hole where my wallowing in self-pity would at least have a larger benefit to mankind. Instead, I had settled in one of the globe's most self-indulgent towns, where I still lacked the courage to fling myself into debauchery wholesale. I stumbled through my days sullen and unapproachable, making sure everyone understood that I had grappled with some larger moral dilemma, even if I didn't bother to explain what it was.

But worse, I began to regard my departure not only as pointless, but as a loathsome bit of self-pity. Regret could have taken any number of forms, but I had chosen the one assured to draw the most attention to myself. I had made sure everyone saw that I was limping as I left the field of battle. Without me, though, the fight had continued on.

I wanted back in. I realized that my reaction had been exactly, precisely wrong. I hadn't caused her death; my advice, in fact, had been pretty good, although delivered badly. But I had seen blood on the battlefield and walked away in horror. The battle didn't end, of course, didn't even slow much, so even as I squatted down out of sight I could hear it continuing without me. Traveling far from the fight hadn't helped. It was perversely curious that my own suggestion to others—just leave—had become an ailment instead of a cure. I had left. That would be excused only when I returned.

So I trained. I would build stamina and will. When I walked into my next newsroom, I would be a weapon. Tough. Alert. Hardy. Woe be unto him who gave me cause to unsheath the sword.

■

I left the way I arrived, with everything loosely packed in two mismatched suitcases and a few cardboard boxes. I had accumulated nothing in eighteen months, and in fact had shed a few things: pounds, mostly, but doubts, too. I was loaded and aimed.

On my way back in the house for the last load, I found Mrs. Reynolds waiting on the porch.

"You ain't going anywhere 'til I count the silverware," she said.

"It wasn't worth stealing," I said. "Pawnshops prefer spoons that actually got washed occasionally."

She grinned. "Are we even on the rent?"

"Pretty much. Unless I get a rebate for having dressed up the place."

"Nah, you're not that delicious," she said. "But I hate to have you go before things are straight in my mind."

It was early and I wasn't going far, so I didn't mind the delay. I settled into a chair.

"What things?"

"Who was the letter from?"

"What letter?"

"What do you mean, what letter?" she asked with exasperation. "The only letter you've gotten the whole time you've been here."

"It was from my grandfather," I said.

She waited a moment for me to say more, then decided I needed a prompt: "Yeah, and . . . ?"

"So I'm supposed to just tell you everything?"

"Who else you gonna tell? All your pals that hang around here day and night?"

"I've got all the friends I need."

She ignored me. "So what did Grandpa say?"

"It was about my mother."

"Oh dear. What happened? Did she die?"

"Sort of. Her good sense did."

"She's crazy?"

"She's been in and out of the state mental hospital for years. He was writing to tell me she's been sent back. She may be there a long time. Maybe permanently."

"Where's your daddy?"

"Buried somewhere. I never knew him. She barely knew him. He was killed in the war."

I could feel her studying me. "No grandma? Just the three of you?"

"That's right."

"And you really hate them."

I considered just walking to the car and driving away. But her questions were so direct and unabashed that they seemed unintrusive, as perversely detached as a pathologist's curiosity as he peels back the flesh and probes for the body's secrets. Besides, her kindness had earned her a certain privilege.

"Maybe I do," I said. "I'm not sure. I'm angry at them for different reasons and that anger won't go away. It squats on the edge of my mind and draws me in. It seems like everything I do is somehow rooted in it."

"What are you angry about?"

"Well, I'm mad at my grandfather for not being a prick anymore."

"Yeah, I always hate it when people turn good," Mrs. Reynolds said.

"No, I mean it," I said. "He was a prick all through my childhood. Mean clear through. I used to wonder what I had done to make him dislike me so much. But there was an odd benefit in it. Kids need to sense an order to the universe, and my grandfather clearly was darkness and evil. It was one of the sure things in my life. I used to dream about him creeping around the house at night, looking into rooms. That's how much he scared me. But when I got older, he stopped being a prick. Or at least I realized that perhaps he'd never really been one, that he was just a guy who'd made bad choices in life and hadn't lived with the consequences very gracefully. That's when I started to really hate him. Because it meant my torment wasn't even deliberate. It was the result of thoughtlessness and carelessness, which is infinitely worse."

"If he was the darkness, who was the good? Your mother?"

"No. She was a void. The happy part of my world was a little crossroads store near my house. I got treated like a regular kid there. The owner was the kindest man I ever knew."

I was quiet for a moment, but Mrs. Reynolds sensed she need not prompt me further. She knew that once the siphoning had begun, it would continue on its own until the supply was gone.

"I'm mad at my mother because I'm her only comfort. She's been unhappy as long as I can remember, but I can't remember a single thing she's ever done about it. Except share it with me."

So I told her. I told her about my whole uncertain, half-breed life. I told her about a lifetime of lingering on the edges, listening in on other people's conversations. I told her about the stacking of words, this way and that, as things happened within my sight but increasingly beyond my feeling. I told her about a woman who called and had the bad luck to remind me of my mother.

I talked until the sun had cleared the top of the palm trees and begun to infect the porch. When I finally stopped, Mrs. Reynolds applied her Conch sensibilities.

"Well, sweets," she said, "all that is why God invented rum."

■

I wonder if I should tell her how wrong I was. I could drive to Key West in a day, provided I started early and remembered to get off the interstate at Fort Pierce and use the turnpike to skirt a hundred miles of congestion. If I ate while I drove and judiciously flouted the speed limit, I could be through Homestead by late afternoon and in Key West by sunset. We could settle into familiar seats on her porch and I could set things right: My grandfather hadn't deserved the revisionist memory I'd awarded him, and my mother wasn't nearly the passive soul whose helplessness had tormented me.

But character is nothing if not consistent. I'd misjudged reality all along. Even though the evidence was scattered everywhere—literally spread about the yard—I'd missed it. I held fast to my notions of things until Jack the dog visited in a dream to jar them loose.

■

I was prey.

Journalists love a mystery, and no more so than when it involves one of their own. The chase began shortly after I left Barrington, when a writer for one of the national journalism reviews called the *Chronicle* to talk to me and ended up with Cooley on the phone.

"I don't know where he is," Cooley said. "He left."

"Where'd he go?" the writer asked.

"To hell, I hope, for leaving me here to answer his goddamn calls," Cooley said.

The writer then somehow got my grandfather's phone number and called at the precise moment when he'd stepped out of the house, leaving my mother alone to answer the call. After years of bizarre letters and whispered phone conversations, it must have seemed providential that someone had finally paid attention.

"Mrs. Beckman?"

"Yes?" my mother replied. It may have been the first time anyone had ever phoned her and certainly the first time anyone had addressed her by the name she'd only briefly worn.

"I'm calling about your son."

"Oh, thank you," she said. "My baby's gone, you see, someone came in the night and took him away. It's a terrible thing, but no one will believe me . . . "

She'd finally gotten her chance to tell her tale, and she wasn't going to be stopped. It came boiling out of her in a long, confused monologue, despite the writer's several attempts to interrupt to make sure he had the right person. Even after my grandfather returned from his walk down the drive to check the mail and wrestled the phone away, she continued to shout out the details, leaving the writer thoroughly bewildered as he heard the commotion and then the abrupt click as my grandfather hung up the phone. He called back but got no answer, neither then nor several other times over the next two days.

Eventually, my grandfather picked up the phone.

"Is Mrs. Beckman there?" the writer asked.

"Who?" my grandfather said. "Tad's married?"

"He is? Maybe I should just call his wife," the writer said, no doubt feeling himself sinking into another conversational morass. "Do you have that number?"

"Whose number?"

The writer tried starting over. "I'm looking for Tad Beckman."

"He doesn't live here."

"Yes, sir, I knew that. I actually wanted to talk to his mother. I think I had her on the phone the other day, but we—" the writer paused "—uh, got cut off."

"She's not here," my grandfather said.

"Will she be in later?"

"I doubt it," my grandfather said, then hung up.

The writer didn't want much. His magazine did a report each year on the new crop of Pulitzer prize winners, and he simply needed a few minutes of my time. I was only one of a couple of dozen people from whom he needed basic biographical information and a single pithy quote suggesting that without journalism, this might have been the year when darkness and evil finally triumphed. But as with any good reporter, his inability to find me only fueled his determination to do so.

He worked the telephone for several days. The tone had already been set by Cooley, my mother and my grandfather, all of whom were perfectly in character when the writer called; but some benign, temporary dementia seemed to have settled upon others, meaning that every conversation the writer had as he pursued me added more evidence to the notion that my world was a strange place, indeed.

"Nah, I haven't seen him in a while," Almo Hardy said. "And it's a good thing, too."

"Why?" the writer asked.

"I've run out of stories about my finger. I'm starting to repeat them."

"What's the matter with your finger?"

"It got cut off."

"What happened?"

"A train ran it over," Almo said.

"A train ran it over?" the writer repeated.

"Sliced it off clean. I keep it here in a big jar of pickles on the counter. Nobody's eaten it yet, so you could come see it if you like."

"How can a train just run over your finger?"

"Well, I was resting it on the track one day and I didn't notice that the train was coming."

"What do you mean you were resting it?"

"Don't your fingers ever get tired?" Almo asked. "Considering your line of work, I would think so."

"Yeah, I suppose," the writer said. "But it wouldn't occur to me to rest them on a railroad track."

"You ought to consider it," Almo said helpfully. "It's usually a pretty good spot. Nice and smooth and warm. Just be sure you listen for the train, though."

By this point, finding me would have ruined what was shaping up to be a marvelous magazine article. So the writer stopped trying, instead spending two months lobbying his editors for permission to come South and untangle this marvelous little mystery in person. The editors were mindful of their meager budget and aware of any reporter's tendency to be promiscuous with other people's money, but they eventually agreed, prompting the writer to fly to Atlanta, rent a car and spend three days poking around Barrington and Doralee, making detailed notes on their quaint characters and customs, and carefully avoiding anything that might actually lead him to me. He even stopped at Almo's store and demanded to see the finger in the pickle jar.

"Aw, I was just kidding you," Almo said. "That train thing never happened."

"Well, then, how did you lose it?" the writer asked.

Almo gave him a droopy-eyed, deadpan look. "Fire ants chewed it off," he said.

It isn't clear whether the writer knocked on the door of my grandfather's house. If he did, and got no answer, there's a reason: My grandfather was gone, arranging for the last of my mother's involuntary commitments. Rousted from their slumber by the writer's telephone call, my mother's shadows had surged forward, using those weeks to permanently claim the territory they had only visited before. This was the shadows' last sally, and it was launched with a vigor and fortitude that made them resistant to any flanking. Their victory eventually proved complete; she never returned home.

Even had he been at home when the writer knocked, it's not likely my grandfather would have heard. He'd taken to spending much of his time in the garden and the yard, the neighbors later reported, tending to his shrubs and vegetables. His hours were often peculiar, they said; he seemed to prefer to work after dusk or in the half-light of early morning. But they attached no importance to it, privately believing that madness was infectious, that Collie's affliction had somehow migrated. These eccentric gardening habits continued for a long time, until someone realized it had been a few days since anyone had seen him. His body was found only twenty-five steps from the back door, still gripping a shovel.

For all his work, one neighbor later noted, the grounds didn't look very good.

■

The article was hilarious. I say that with no small bit of envy.

WHERE IN THE WORLD IS TAD BECKMAN? the headline asked. Underneath, in smaller letters, a second headline set the tone: "A Pulitzer prize winner disappears, leaving our correspondent to sort out the mystery. Where did he go? Whose baby is gone? And what really happened to that fellow's finger?"

Of course, the writer didn't sort out anything. He served up a lazy accounting of the events leading to my departure, plundering my column and the *Chronicle*'s reporting for the meat of it, then made himself the central character in a tale of travel through the gothic South. But his touch was sure. He avoided the usual clichés, resisting the years-of-inbreeding-gives-us-this attitude to which many Northern visitors succumb, and instead made himself the rube, wandering about the landscape and being bested by the canny locals, who offer only epigrammatic clues to my life. The article ran longer than his magazine usually preferred, and was clearly out of character with its usual diet of scoldings of inept journalism and collections of absurd and nonsensical headlines. But its good-natured humor made it irresistible, both to the review's readers and to the editors of *The New York Times,* who bought the rights to reprint the article. So on a Sunday just a few months after I had convinced Mrs. Reynolds of my fully committed heterosexuality, the *Times* unveiled me as the latest in a line of distinctly American creations: the momentary media sensation.

When I finally read the article, it should have been an object lesson in the treacherous nature of appearances. The writer was later hung by his own words. He'd seen only what he wanted to see, believed it when he saw it and written it well, which is a combustible mixture. If you're going to take on faith what you see, there's a peculiar salvation in bad writing. At least it will be ignored when it's revealed the faith was ill-placed.

But it was lost to me as a lesson. Worse yet, when I later made the same mistake myself, I could perversely trace it back to this writer. I hadn't been his prey, you see. He was merely Lady, flushing me from the thicket and pointing me out to the actual hunter.

■

You don't read in exile, especially a self-imposed one.

I missed the article, both in its original form and in the *Times*'s reprinting. The writer had borrowed a photograph of me from the Barrington *Chronicle,* after agreeing to Cooley's demand that it not be returned and in fact preferably be destroyed, but if anyone in Key West saw my image and made the connection between the tortured, missing columnist depicted in the article and the occasionally surly local barkeep who was notable for little more than his utter lack of success in getting laid even in a place where an oversupply of queer men culled the competition dramatically, no one mentioned it.

So my reception at the *Post-Star* was a surprise. I'd left Mrs. Reynolds's boardinghouse that morning with an even dozen identical envelopes on the rear seat of the car, each of them stuffed with the requisite job-hunting ammunition: résumé, copies of my better news stories and columns, and a one-page biography that assiduously avoided the mention of the Pulitzer prize and its circumstances. My plan was to drop the envelopes off at a selected twelve newspapers between Miami and Atlanta, then wait to see who—if anyone—called.

But I got no further than the *Post-Star*'s lobby.

I had hoped to hand the envelope personally to the editor,

perhaps catching his ear and eye and thereby avoiding the likelihood of simply being added to the stack of hundreds of similar applications that surely lived in a secretary's drawer. But I was foiled by Emile, a hard-eyed Haitian who wore the uniform of a private security firm and manned the visitors desk with an immigrant's seriousness.

"He's not in," Emile said after a perfunctory call to another phone somewhere in the building. He waited for me to declare my intentions.

"Can I leave this with you, then?" I asked. "You'll see that he gets it?"

"I will ensure your package is delivered to the editor," he said, formal and purposeful.

A young woman passing by at that moment heard his promise. "I'm going up, Emile. I'll take it," she said. Wordlessly, he handed it over and she clacked away, hardly breaking stride at the exchange.

I lingered in the lobby. The *Post-Star,* having succumbed to the notion that a newspaper should be happy and friendly, in its home as well as in its pages, had made its foyer into a miniature art gallery. It was a spacious and airy place, with twenty-foot windows looking out at Biscayne Bay and a marble floor that somehow stayed cool even as the Florida sun burned through the glass, fixtures typical of a company that wishes to demonstrate that its wealth and power are so vast it can afford a costly, useless public area. On one side of Emile's post stood a collection of wheeled display boards covered with children's artwork and accompanied by a sign announcing that this exhibit was courtesy of the Liberation Preschool Academy of South Miami. On the other side was a matching set of display boards covered with photographs, an apparent shrine to the better efforts of the *Post-Star*'s staff photographers. I chose that side.

It was a clever and educational effort. For each featured photograph, there was a copy of the newspaper page where it had originally appeared and an enlarged copy of the contact sheet that showed the other photographs of the same subject that had not made publication. A sign explained the role of the *Post-Star*'s photo editor and invited viewers to examine the rejected photographs and second-guess his judgment.

I was studying the collection when I heard Emile's phone ring. He listened for a moment, then said, "Yes, he's still here." He listened for another long moment, then hung up.

"Sir?" he called. When I looked up, he beckoned me to his desk.

"Would you mind waiting a moment, sir?" he said, suddenly more solicitous. "Someone is on his way down to see you."

I didn't get to finish my study of the photographs. But I had dallied long enough for the memory of one of the pictures to burrow deep into my subconsciousness. It hid there for over a year, whispering to me occasionally to make me look its way, then skittering out of sight before I could capture it. When I finally seized it and dragged it into the light, it was too late.

■

"Tad Beckman?"

A distinguished old gentleman bustled across the lobby toward me, hand extended. "Tad?" he asked again. "I'm Al Manzini."

He seemed to want me to recognize the name, and after a moment it clicked. "I took your advice," I said, "and look where it got me: Fifteen years later, I'm still begging for work."

He laughed, obviously pleased that I remembered. "I've still got that letter somewhere. Funniest goddamn thing I ever read. So tell me," he said, turning serious. "Where have you been?"

"Barrington, Georgia," I said. "The *Chronicle*."

"Jesus, I know that. Everybody knows that." His speech had the impatient cadence of that of a native New Yorker. "Where have you been lately?"

"Key West."

"Damn. I should listen to my instincts," he said. "I wondered if you weren't there after I read the *Times* piece. Considered having our guy there nose around. But I decided you'd headed for the frontier. Alaska or something."

"What *Times* piece?"

He gave me an incredulous look. "You don't know this?" I thought suddenly of Almo Hardy, telling me of my mother's madness.

"Know what?"

"About your disappearance."

"What disappearance? I just moved. I didn't know I was supposed to check in with someone."

Manzini lifted his eyes to the ceiling. "Thank you, Lord," he said.

The other eleven envelopes became trash. We spent the afternoon negotiating the details, with salary coming easily but the telling of my recent months proving nettlesome. Manzini wanted the first column to recount my departure, but I could see where that led; besides, I said, I hadn't written the silly, overblown tale that the *Times* had reprinted, and felt no need to bear the burden of correcting it.

"I'm not going to undress again," I declared. "I did it once. That's all anyone gets."

Manzini eventually claimed that position as his own. As would any good manager, he appropriated my moral qualm and waited only a few minutes before making it a policy edict, staking out the high ground and inviting me to join him there.

"Prefer not to have you write it, if you don't mind," he said. "I'm going to put someone else on this. You can come out of the gate with something else. You'll need a few days to settle in, right? Let's start you . . . let's see, Ray's usually in on Sundays. Next weekend?"

"Who's Ray?" I asked.

I got a glimpse of the sword, and suddenly felt sorry for the writer who set all this into motion. "He used to be our columnist, but I'm tired of reading about his kids. I think a little time in Hialeah will do him good."

■

My pity was well placed. On the day my first column ran, the *Post-Star* also offered a story headlined WRITER "FOUND," BUT WAS NEVER LOST. It was a merciless debunking. The reporter— one of the Dobermans Manzini kept on staff precisely for this sort of assignment—noted, among other things, that I had filed a forwarding address with the Barrington post office, and that a simple letter would have found its way to me in Key West. Also, a name or two had been muddled in the original piece and my mother's affliction had been treated cavalierly, making her debilitating psychosis seem like a gentle bit of country quirkiness. All that left the *Post-Star* with the opportunity to paint the writer as being careless and cruel on top of just plain wrong, and Manzini seized it.

I stayed clear of the brawl that resulted. *The New York Times,* finding itself in the unhappy position of defending a piece it hadn't originated, sought to distance itself from the writer even as it embraced what it declared was an "essential truth" in his effort. That sent Manzini—who, as it turned out, carried a legendary grudge against the *Times* for its failure some years before to promote him, a bit of insight that made me understand his thanks to the heavens that afternoon in the lobby—into his office for two days to craft a tortured broadside explaining that the latest point on the line through history that connects every great human failing now included this insidious defense of something called essential truth. "Its very invocation by the *Times,* a paper alleged to be great, mostly by people who don't read it, may well undermine the public trust enjoyed by smaller newspapers, whose employees rarely encounter diplomats, statesmen and celebrities, but see their ordinary, hardworking neighbors every day—neighbors who, unencumbered by the need to dress up their language as art-fully as the *Times* has when it calls a skein of distortions 'es-sential truth,' likely will ask, as they bump into these more modest journalists at the store or see them over the fence in the backyard, how the devil newspapers ever got to the point when scrupulous accuracy was a disposable commodity," Manzini wrote. He was not a man given to subtlety, or periods. That was one of his shorter sentences.

Over the next few weeks, other editors weighed in with their own pompous observations. Ultimately, *The New Yorker* put a coda on the whole affair by sending one of its smarmier writers out to summarize it. She opened her piece by declaring, "As most readers of daily newspapers eventually discover, journal-ism is a shell game and truth is the pea, rarely uncovered and then only grudgingly by those who control the game." This, mind you, from a magazine that for most of its history refused to print corrections or even letters from anyone who might want to uncover the pea themselves.

The hostilities faded a short time later and the combatants left the field. The body count was relatively modest: The writer who began the whole thing was fired from the journalism re-view, while the *Times* editor who had reprinted the piece was called into a private office and slapped around. Manzini com-plained that the blood should have run more deeply, but he ac-cepted the one scalp he'd taken and hung it on his belt.

"Would you have answered if he'd written?" he asked me later.

"Probably not," I said.

"Do you think he sensed that?"

"Probably so."

"So this guy loses his job because he didn't do something he knew would be fruitless."

"So it seems," I said.

Manzini smirked. "Tough world," he said.

■

As I said, justice tripped me up. But breasts were certainly a contributing cause.

Here's how you can see the most abundant display of innocent, wholesome, mostly unclothed breasts in America: Catch any commercial airline flight to Miami, then take the MacArthur Causeway to Miami Beach; park as close to Ocean Drive as possible in any one of the six or so available parking spaces in the whole city; find Tenth Street and follow it east until it dead-ends at the beach; then walk out onto the sand and drink in nature's bounty. Your pale skin and slack-jawed look will doubtless give you away as a tourist, but if you smoke a lot of cigarettes and avoid bathing for a few days beforehand, everyone will assume you're European. It's better that way: What looks like a leer on the face of an American tourist is considered savoir faire in a Frenchman.

Or you can do what I did. You can take a small apartment in a past-its-prime Art Deco building in South Beach—a place cooled by dripping air conditioners in windows and largely populated by retirees who wear sweaters even in August as they sit on the terrace—and wait for someone to come along and help you finish the job of making a complete wreck of your life.

CHAPTER EIGHT

It's not as if Adele Bickerstaff didn't know the alligator was there.

After all, she'd seen it any number of times at the lake across the road from her apartment. Actually, it's not a lake as much as it is a wide spot in one of the countless canals that thread across South Florida. But if you're an apartment building owner and you've advertised "lakeside living," you'd better have something to show people. And if you're Mrs. Bickerstaff and you've told all your friends back in Cleveland, Ohio, that you're living the good life on the waterfront, it ought to be more than a canal.

So everybody calls it a lake, except the alligator. He calls it home.

It's also not as if Mrs. Bickerstaff didn't know, in a vague way, that alligators eat other animals. She sort of remembers watching a television show one night that showed animals hunting one another—among them an alligator bagging a duck or something. Besides, anyone can see they're huge and scary-looking, not the sort of beast that munches peacefully on grass.

But this alligator didn't seem dangerous. She would walk Benny, her toy poodle, along the lake and occasionally see the alligator on the bank, yet all it ever did was sit motionless. The first couple of times, Benny would strain against the leash and *bark*—Let me at this guy, I'll show him a thing or two—*and she would cut a wide path around the creature. Eventually, though, both Benny and Mrs. Bickerstaff grew accustomed to seeing it.*

All parties happily coexisted until the day the alligator ate Benny.

It was quick and brutal, Mrs. Bickerstaff recalls. There was Benny, sniffing innocently in the tall grass at the edge of the water, when suddenly the alligator lunged open-mouthed out of the water in a wet blur. In a single horrible movement, the alligator swallowed Benny whole, snapped his head to pull the leash away, and somehow backpedaled into the water again. The last evidence of Benny's existence was the sight of the leash trailing behind the alligator as it swam away to chew and digest privately.

As you might imagine, it was terrifying and traumatizing. After an initial period of hysteria, Mrs. Bickerstaff took to her bed, depressed and lonely. When she stirred herself a week later, she found comfort and therapy in that uniquely American pastime: She filed a lawsuit.

This is where things get strange. When you file a lawsuit, you have to name a specific person, company or institution as the cause of your problem. Mrs. Bickerstaff could have sued the alligator, I suppose, but depositions and other routine court proceedings would have been tricky. She considered suing the South Florida Water Management District, which maintains the canal, but her lawyer decided it's best not to tangle with a quasi-government body that keeps attorneys permanently on call for exactly this kind of dispute.

So after much debate and deep reflection, Mrs. Bickerstaff and her lawyer realized who was truly at fault for Benny's death: The Lakeside Homeowners Association, the governing body of the complex where she lives.

The lawsuit claims the association negligently failed to explain to Mrs. Bickerstaff all the possible bad things that could happen to her if she moved to the complex. It was clear to the association that Mrs. Bickerstaff was from Cleveland, a place notably short on alligators, and so it should have taken the trouble to tell her to stay far, far away from them. It didn't, and therefore is responsible for Benny's death, the lawsuit claims.

Because the association is overseen by a board of directors, each board member is named individually in the lawsuit. Interestingly, the board president—whose name appears at the top of the lawsuit—lives next door to Mrs. Bickerstaff, and in fact was the first to stop by with a pie when she moved in.

In other words, Mrs. Bickerstaff is suing her neighbor because her dog was eaten by an alligator on somebody else's property a quarter mile away.

There are some natural questions that arise from all this. For instance, is there no case so goofy that a lawyer somewhere won't take it? Is there still any uncertainty as to why our court system is clogged beyond all clearing? Is it wrong to wish that every small, annoying dog be taken for a walk along an alligator-infested canal?

I'd like to dwell on these issues awhile, but I can't. I need to go talk to my neighbor now.

I need to explain to her why it's a bad thing to jam the pointed end of a golf tee deep into your ear. And why it's unwise to lick the inside of your freezer. And why you shouldn't use a stapler to remove a stray eyelash. And why . . .

Well, you get the idea.

Miami is full of rogues, thieves, scoundrels, wastrels, plotters and pretenders. And that's just a look at its business and civic leaders.

It proved to be a columnist's paradise. It is a land of second chances, the place where people who have made a hash of their finances, marriages, political situations or standing as law-abiding citizens flee to so that they can make a better run at things. Or at least not get caught this time.

It is a place where the owner of a mansion is a Latin immigrant who speaks broken English while the groundskeeper is
white and American-born; where a judge can ease his worries
about funding his children's college education by selling the
name of a confidential informant to a drug dealer who will
make sure the informant informs no more; where high-rise
bank buildings stand only blocks from crowded, exotic shop-
ping districts where English will get you ignored and the absence of herds of goats is your only clue that you're not in some
Third World city; where the fellow who runs the lunch counter
around the corner from your office was commanding some
Central American government's death squad only a few years
prior; where the mayor acknowledges that freedom of speech is
an honored concept, unless the speech even hints that an accommodation of Castro is inevitable, in which case bloodlet-
ting is the approved result; where you actually see refugees
arrive with only change in their pockets and prove that this is a
land of opportunity by becoming millionaires in just a few
years; where a 100,000-bulb Christmas display in front of your
home is considered tasteful and reverent; where the organized-
crime figure named in the recent indictment lives just down the
street but no one cares because he gives out the best candy at
Halloween and besides, the Colombians have redefined the image of gangsters, making the old-style mob guys and their gam-
bling rackets seem quaint and nostalgic; and where, in a single
ten-minute drive, you could make yourself believe you've
landed in a suburb of New York, Tel Aviv, Havana or Port-au-
Prince.

It also turned out to be what I had hoped for in Key West: a
place that lives in the present. In Miami, all history belongs to
other places. Nothing is rooted there. The people all come from
somewhere else, the homes are simply set atop concrete slabs,
even the vegetation pulls up easily from the sandy soil, happy
to be just jammed into the ground again somewhere else.

So I didn't have to ease into my role. I took a great, conspicuous swan dive into the first available issue—the trial of a black store owner who had killed a young, white would-be robber under questionable circumstances and now faced an ambitious Cuban prosecutor in front of a mercurial, controversial Jewish judge, one of those great only-in-Miami events that cuts across every racial and ethnic fault line—and from that moment forward I was part of the landscape. I settled into both an apartment on Miami Beach and the newsroom culture, finding an easy acceptance in each place. I got into the habit of lifting a half-dozen papers from the newsroom stack as I left each evening and dropping them on the table in the lobby of my apartment building; my neighbors, almost all of them retirees, soon took a larcenous glee in canceling their newspaper subscriptions and instead gathering every night to quibble over the sections and repeat their chronic complaints that some among them tended to dawdle over the comics or sports.

At work, my colleagues overcame their suspicions that I had somehow engineered the exile of my predecessor to Hialeah and realized that I could perform a unique function for them: I could state baldly what they could only hint at in their reports. So if a certain city official, a notably inept fool, made a hash of his office's transition to a new computer system and all property tax bills went out late as a result, the reporter's news story necessarily carried the city's official explanation that the new equipment had proven to be unreasonably balky, but that kinks were being worked out. However, I could declare that the city official had ignored the advice of underlings who'd warned him that this system was a proven plague in other offices, and that he'd apparently recommended its purchase only because the sales representative had a provocative roll to her hips, laughed at his bawdy jokes and patiently honored his repeated requests for yet one more demonstration of her wares. In short, I could reveal that he was not only a notably inept fool, but a horny old goat as well.

I was wearing my life well within months. I was a swashbuckling smuggler of newspapers to my neighbors and the back-channel carrier of pertinent but awkward information for my colleagues. I lacked only two things: a crusade and a woman.

One, as it turned out, would bring the other.

■

I don't remember the day I first saw her. In cities, you don't notice what's new; you notice what's no longer new. So for a long time—or for what seemed like a long time, but in reality was probably only a month or two—she was just an occasional part of an ever-changing landscape: a face at the corner, at the beach, at the market, inscrutable and a bit severe behind sunglasses.

But one day the face smiled faintly as we stood together at a crosswalk. A few days later it happened again, but that time the smile was certain.

"Morning," I said. She nodded a greeting, then looked away and crossed the street.

It was only then that she registered in my consciousness. I noticed that from a block away, she was twenty-five; from a half-block away, she was thirty; and next to her on the sidewalk, she was in her midthirties. But the clues were not to be found in her face or shape, where men typically search, but in her hands and eyes, where a faint network of lines had begun to form but were visible only in the unforgiving Florida sun.

I refined the image over the next several encounters. Her hair was dark and a bit unkempt, held in place by a variety of devices pinned randomly to her head in different spots every day, but not suggesting slovenliness as much as an acknowledgment that the incessant beach breeze would foil any more complicated effort. She wore casual clothes in interesting combinations—for instance, an oversized, mannish white shirt rolled at the sleeves, covered by a linen vest liberated from a secondhand clothes shop; or a long, billowy earth-mother skirt with a hump-me tank top—meaning that if she worked, it wasn't in a place with a particularly scrupulous dress code. She walked purposefully and always wore low shoes, in contrast to the virgin-whore look peculiar to Miami that prompts its women to wear spike heels in innocent settings. Her body was thicker than men think they like, until they discover that what looks large feels lush.

She drew attention, even though South Florida is a place that accommodates the old, honors the young and embraces the hustler, and she was none of those. At least, she drew attention from me.

Then one day she suddenly appeared next to me on the beach.

"Hi," she said abruptly. I was sitting on a towel watching people play in the surf, and was startled when she came up behind me.

"Hello," I said. I stood and immediately felt foolishly formal, then compounded it by reaching out to shake hands.

"Hi," she said again, ignoring my hand. "Listen, some creep down the beach was bothering me. Do you mind if I sit with you for a while?"

"Sure. Absolutely." I gazed down the beach, trying to look menacing and competent. "Where is he?"

"He won't bother us. He's probably a tourist. Seemed harmless, but he just wouldn't go away. I told him I was supposed to meet my boyfriend, but he didn't take the hint. So when I noticed you, I said, 'Oh, there he is,' and came over. I hope you don't mind."

"No, it's fine. Glad I could help."

She held her towel by the corners and snapped it once, then spread it on the sand next to mine. We both sat down.

"Hi," she said for a third time. "I'm Jocelyn."

"Tad," I said, reaching out my hand again. That time she shook it.

She was quiet for a few moments, then said, "You must live around here. I've seen you a few times, haven't I?"

"Yeah, I'm around."

"What do you do?"

"I work at the *Post-Star*," I said, running the words together as most locals did. *Postar.*

"Oh? As what?"

"Columnist."

"What's your name again?"

"Tad Beckman."

It obviously didn't register. "Sorry," she said, shaking her head. "I haven't been around long enough to know the paper."

It was my turn: "What do you do?"

"I'm a refugee," she said flatly, inviting no further questions.

About twenty feet away, a young mother sitting with her infant son under an umbrella began changing his diaper. We watched as the child, temporarily naked on the blanket, waved his arms with a baby's spasticity until he inadvertently found his genitals. He was still for a moment as his eyes widened comically.

Jocelyn turned her attention back to me. "And thus begins another lifelong love affair," she said.

How was I to resist this woman?

■

She made sure I didn't.

The next weekend, I returned to the beach. I had not seen her in days, despite several long, aimless walks through Miami Beach's Art Deco neighborhood. I didn't know where she lived. We'd sat on our towels for an hour that first day, talking and watching for the creep, before she'd suddenly begun gathering her things and declaring she was late for something, leaving me with a hurried "Listen, thanks a million" over her shoulder. Cooler then, I didn't get off my towel. Just another day for Tad

Beckman, rescue and protection specialist. "See you," I said casually. Regret took root within minutes.

So I had trudged through the neighborhood in the evenings after work, lingering at crosswalks and store windows for long minutes in the fading light, or buying a *café con leche* at one of the sidewalk serving windows favored by Cuban restaurants and nursing it as I leaned against the wall and listened to old men argue in Spanish. I hoped for a chance encounter, but it never came. Without much confidence, I tried the beach on Saturday.

She was there, in almost the precise spot we'd shared the week before. She waved me over.

"It's Todd, right?" she said as I approached.

"Tad."

"Ted?"

"Ta-ad." I made it a slow two syllables, the way I'd grown up hearing it.

"Oops. Sorry." She patted the sand next to her. "Have a seat."

I sat and looked around. "Am I your boyfriend again today?"

"Not so far. But we have a whole new wave of visitors, so we'll see."

The beach was indeed crowded with tourists. It was one of those glorious late-winter days that South Florida proffers to balance the scale, to make everyone forgive August's crimes of climate. Also, the city was enjoying a period of calm—riots and boatlifts were behind it, while future riots and boatlifts were still only gestating in local slums and faraway capitals—so European travel agents felt confident enough to send their clients to Miami with the expectation that they actually would return.

Moments after I arrived, a German family laid claim to a nearby patch of sand, dropping towels and toys into a heap and stepping out of clunky street shoes worn unlaced and without socks. The two children immediately headed for the water, while the parents—a beefy Brunhilde and her freckled husband—both lit cigarettes and stripped to their swimsuits, revealing great expanses of already-burned skin and making me wonder where I could place a bet on which cancer would get them first. The woman then did something that was becoming increasingly common on Miami Beach: She unhooked the top half of her suit and let her great, pendulous breasts swing free.

I looked at Jocelyn and she smirked. "Master race likes 'em big, I guess," she said.

"It's no wonder they took over Europe," I said. "They needed the room."

She looked toward the couple again. "You know, I've wondered what the attraction is. You see women doing it all the time now."

I shrugged.

"If I do it, are you gonna stare at my boobs?"

"Stare? Nah," I said. "But I'll probably look out of the corner of my eye a few times."

"How many times?"

"Three?" It was an odd negotiation.

"Two," she said. "And I'll tell you right now, they don't measure up to the competition."

I bargained in bad faith. I looked countless times until the moment she declared, "Well, this is certainly overrated," and slipped into a T-shirt. And she was wrong. They measured up quite nicely.

■

Another day:

"How did you become a refugee?" I asked.

"The usual way. I packed in a hurry and left in the middle of the night."

I tried another tack. "What were you seeking refuge from?"

"Do we have to talk about this?"

"No," I said. "I'm just curious."

We were sitting at an outside table in a café along Ocean Drive, being ignored by a surly waitress who preferred to rest a haunch on the railing at the sidewalk and smoke cigarettes. I had capitalized on my second encounter on the beach, asking for an evening date but settling for coffee in the afternoon at a restaurant she named, which I presumed was near her home. It was only one of the things I set out to discover.

"Have you lived here long?"

"Not long," she said. "A couple of months."

"Where exactly do you live?"

"Just over there," she said, waving her hand vaguely away from the beach.

"Where did you come from?"

"Up the coast a ways. Near Pompano Beach."

"What brought you here?"

She just gave me a flat look.

"This is how a reporter makes conversation," I said. "We're a smooth bunch."

"Sorry," she said, softening a bit. "I'm just embarrassed about it."

"About what?"

"I'll tell you. But you've got to promise me one thing."

"What?"

"That you won't feel sorry for me. I'm not a victim."

∎

It was another ordinary story.

There was again an abusive husband, violence and visits by the police. There was again a long period during which she avoided certain topics, certain clothes, certain people, assuming that if she sidestepped the points of conflict, there would be no conflict. But she found that accommodation is treacherous. The calm that followed each concession merely disguised the movement of explosive mines to new territory, giving him time to brush the earth carefully to hide them before she blundered in anew. As she talked, I heard echoes of a previous conversation.

But there were differences, too. It was not a trailer park this time, but a half-million-dollar home on a deep-water canal, the sort of place upon which whole industries are built: landscaping, pool maintenance, domestic service. And the husband wasn't a drunken layabout, but a respected builder and developer, a man who played in every charitable golf tournament and always checked the box that said "Reserve my table for ten" when civic groups sent invitations to their annual dinners. And there were no children, no neighbors, no witnesses.

There was one other important difference: There was no helplessness.

"I fought him to a draw, most times," she said. "He had this odd sense of propriety about it. He wouldn't hit me with anything but his hand. But I'd smack him with anything I could grab. I got him a few good times with a meat tenderizer. You know those hammerlike things you pound meat with? I kept one handy most of the time. I'd buy tough cuts of meat just to have an excuse to have it out on the kitchen counter."

She'd also taken the advice I gave someone else. She finally just left.

"But I didn't want to leave with nothing. So I spent a few weeks selling all the things I knew he wouldn't notice were gone. Stuff like my Rolex and some artwork we had stored away. I also stopped paying all the bills and diverted the money over to an account I opened. Then one morning I withdrew all that money, and took everything out of our joint accounts, and just drove away."

"Did you leave him a note or anything?" I asked.

"Sort of. I took his Hermès ties and cut them up into a bunch of little pieces. You know what I'm talking about, those ties that cost about a hundred bucks apiece? He must have had thirty of them. I used the pieces to leave a trail from the door to the kitchen, like one of those lines you see in hospitals that some bossy nurse tells you to follow to get somewhere. And there on the kitchen counter I had every past-due notice laid out for him. Every bill was at least three months overdue. The bank was foreclosing on the house, his golf club was cutting him off, everything. In fact, the power got turned off that day. I had to open all the drapes so he would be sure to see the trail. I'll bet it was a furnace when he opened the door." She grinned happily at the memory.

"Are you divorced now?"

"Not yet. Papers are filed, but he's being difficult. It took him a while to climb out of the hole I left him in. He eventually did, though. Now he's got a high-priced lawyer who's steam-rolling over my attorney." She became subdued. "He's even talking to prosecutors about whether I can be charged with taking the money."

"What's your husband's name? Have I ever heard of him?"

"You will. Laney Pritchard. He's about to buy your apartment building and tear it down."

■

Let's review: She was married. Her husband was prone to violence. She was in the middle of a contentious divorce, living off money a court might decide was stolen. And Laney Pritchard's plans for a new development threatened my own home, an issue that became critically important later on.

Any reasonable man would have been looking for the emergency exit. I fell in love.

We left the restaurant, and as we walked away her hand found mine. That afternoon, I indeed discovered where she lived: discovered the street, the building and the apartment. I discovered a chair in her bedroom on which clothes could be draped. I discovered anew the change in shape and color that flesh undertakes as it signals its desires. I discovered a window above our heads that could be opened to the breeze as we lay together, overheated and humid.

Tell me how I should have known. Tell me what I should have seen. Tell me why I shouldn't have reveled in my good fortune and feasted on the great, lush handfuls of her.

Here's your answer: Once a man smells a woman on him, his other senses flee.

■

But there's another reason, too. My love life hadn't played host to good fortune on many prior occasions.

I was wholly unfamiliar with the role of happy lover. Until then, romance had been an obstacle course designed by a perfectly demented mind. My overtures to women were accepted only tentatively, my gestures were late and clumsy, my instincts were flawed, and my tendency to treat a relationship as a connected series of advances, as a strategic exercise, was all too apparent. I was promiscuous in a way men typically aren't: I would commit to anyone who would have me, even if I couldn't understand why she would want me. That combination of fervor and uncertainty, along with my constant need to see tangible proof of a relationship's progress, usually had women looking for a way out within weeks.

The treacherous nature of this realm was revealed to me early. When I was sixteen, I developed a longing for a girl in my class at Doralee High School. We'd been assigned to several classes together, and thanks to a school policy that assigned book lockers on an alphabetic basis, we shared the same bit of wall between two rooms. Her name was Abby Burritt, and she was a plain girl who resolutely sought out the desk in the square middle of each classroom and had an unsettling need to hover near homecoming queens and cheerleaders. I had not taken much notice of her in previous years, preferring instead to speculate with my friends about the carnal desires of those very same queens and cheerleaders, but when during the new school term's first week of class she had turned suddenly toward me as we stood together at our lockers and caught me clearly noticing that her blouse was newly and proudly filled— and had given me a look that seemed to my sixteen-year-old eye not only to be not reproving but actually saucy and daring—well, the world suddenly seemed filled with undiscovered possibilities.

So I had undertaken a campaign to woo her. Uncertain as to how exactly to go about it, and unable to ask my mother for advice because she was in one of her periods when she tended to keep to her room, I treated it as an intellectual challenge and began studying. In the school library I found several volumes on manners and etiquette, all of which made at least a passing reference to the mechanics of the relationship between an unmarried man and unmarried woman; and in the Doralee Public Library I found two books that purported to be marriage manuals, although they chiefly seemed to dwell on tactics to avoid "nocturnal emissions" and such. However, one of them had a long chapter on courtship, and despite the book's clear belief that it was to be conducted with the precision and formality of a Viennese waltz, I gleaned some helpful ideas. (Of course, I also learned that caressing my tingly parts would rob me of vigor and moral stability, a notion that dozens of more modern studies could never quite overcome in the following years.)

I became a cheerful and attentive sort. I mined the newspaper each morning for the conversation starter I would need at our first locker encounter of the day. I watched for every opportunity to be helpful with books or to hold open doors. I learned the routines of her day and adjusted my own schedule as best I could to always be nearby when she exited a class or stood in the lunch line. I saw myself as gallant and romantic, and even though that sort of lurking, persistent presence even-

tually would come to be known as stalking, she seemed to like
the attention. So when she accepted my carefully orchestrated
request to be my date at the school's annual homecoming football game and subsequent dance, I was ready to conclude that
romance indeed was something that lent itself to planning and
strategy.

Instead, she turned out to be the first of many catastrophes
of courtship.

I arrived at her home at the appointed hour in my grandfather's car. I had fretted over asking him to use it, and had pretty
much decided just to drive the battered old pickup truck that I
was normally allowed to use, when, in a rare flourish of gen-
erosity, he offered me the sedan. My mother had brightened up
as well, helping me with my clothes and insisting I prove I
knew how to dance by leading her across the kitchen as she
hummed a few of the popular tunes of the day. After a quick
lesson on how to pin a corsage, they had sent me off. I felt confident and happy when I pulled into Abby's drive.

That mood's erosion started almost immediately. Her father
was cool, even surly, while her mother, taking no chances, appropriated the corsage and attached it herself, then smoothed
Abby's dress and murmured something that sounded uncom-
fortably like sympathy. Abby herself had a nervous smile that
clicked on and off at random, and she assured her parents as
we left that she wouldn't be late.

She didn't say much as we drove to the football field, letting
me chatter on about various topics that I had archived to be
withdrawn one by one: new teachers, new television shows, the
sit-in at the Woolworth lunch counter in North Carolina, John
Kennedy's prospects of being elected president the next month.
When I'd exhausted my list and was wondering whether turning on the car radio would signal a conversational defeat, she
finally spoke.

"You didn't tell me you were Jewish," she said, making it
sound like an accusation.

"Well, I'm not, really," I said.

"My dad says you are."

"No, really," I insisted. "I've never even been inside a—" I paused for a moment, certain that using the word "synagogue" would suggest I was all too familiar with the very thing I sought to deny "—a Jewish church."

"He says your father was a Jew," she said, boring in like a prosecutor.

"I've heard the same thing." I gave what I hoped was a rueful grin. "He died. I never knew him."

She seemed only slightly mollified. "I just wish you'd told me, that's all."

When we arrived at the field, I found that she'd made arrangements to join a friend and her date in the stands. We'd been seated only a few moments when Abby decided she and her friend needed to make sure the class float, the decoration of which Abby had supervised, was ready for the halftime parade, in which returning alumni and a half-dozen floats would promenade in front of the stands in the stylized ritual of homecoming. The float, a riot of streamers and papier-mâché that purported to show one of our football heroes cleaving the skull of an enemy player with a tomahawk—we were, after all, the Doralee Braves—had been built on a flatbed trailer that now sat parked behind a truck on the far side of the field. I watched as the two of them tiptoed their way around the end zone, avoiding the soggy spots lest the heels of their new pumps impale themselves into the ground. At one point they stopped and looked back, with the friend waving to her date but Abby taking care not to. They finally reached the float, gave it an inspection casual enough to belie the whole exercise, then made their way back to their seats.

Just as the girls settled back into the gap between me and the other boy, Abby stood again. "I left my purse over there," she said.

"I'll get it," I said. After all, that's what you do when you're gallant and helpful, not to mention a conqueror of nocturnal emissions.

I made my way across the field, found her purse sitting on an edge of the flatbed trailer and headed back for the grandstand. As I drew close, I had to stop for a moment as the school's drill team passed in front of me, marching to a cadence pounded out by the band's drum corps and headed for the tunnel leading from the locker room under the stands. I had seen this countless times before: The girls of the drill team, dressed in bouncy little skirts and white boots with small pompons attached to the fronts, would form two parallel lines stretching from the locker room to the field, then would march in place as the cheerleading squad—cheering madly and running fetchingly in their own bouncy little skirts—led the football team onto the field. The team, inspired by all this twitching and flexing of teenage female thighs, would then mash the other team into the turf, keeping safe our school's honor for another week.

As the end of the drill team passed in front of me, one of the girls gave me a quizzical look from the corner of her eye. I realized I must have looked odd, a lone boy standing on the edge of the field with a purse hooked over his arm. A comical impulse took hold.

I fell in behind the drill team, high-stepping in time to the drumbeat and with hands on hips and elbows out just like the girls. The purse bounced off my leg as I marched, and the laughter from the stands had already started to build when I performed the finale. As each girl in turn reached her assigned spot in the line, she pirouetted ninety degrees and flung her arm diagonally toward the sky, marching all the while and presumably pointing to the heaven that awaits football heroes. When my turn came, I executed a crisp turn and shot my arm out, letting the purse dangle from my fingers.

The crowd roared in approval, sending up such a large cheer that the girls in the front of the line, nearest the locker room, strained to see what had caused the commotion. I maintained my place in line until the football squad had run onto the field, keeping perfect step all the while, then peeled off when the drill team began its march back to its seats. A wave of applause followed me as I climbed through the stands to my own seat.

The crowd may have appreciated my improvisation, but Abby hadn't. I had neglected to consider that a girl who desired the middle desk in each classroom and was happy just to be close to popular students wouldn't enjoy the attention that came with my impromptu bit of slapstick. She edged as far away from me as the crowded bleachers would allow, and her face took on a blush that wouldn't fade, even after the game had begun and everyone's attention focused elsewhere. She had a couple of whispered conversations with her girlfriend, one of which briefly included her girlfriend's date, then she spoke her first words to me since I'd returned with her purse: "I've got to go to the bathroom." The two girls then squeezed by me and disappeared behind the grandstand.

After a long while, the girlfriend came back alone, smiling at me uncertainly as she squeezed back to her seat, but saying nothing. When I finally asked about Abby, the girlfriend said, "I don't think she's feeling well." A short time later, she and her date declared they were off to the concession stand; I eventually saw them sitting in another spot.

Abby never returned. I sat alone for the rest of the game, craning my head back occasionally to look for her but otherwise pretending that she'd only been delayed. When the game concluded and everyone began filing out of the grandstand, I continued to sit, unwilling to believe she had left. It wasn't until the groundskeeper had turned off the lights on the close side of the field and had headed for the far side to do the same that I finally stood to go. That's when I saw my grandfather sitting on the top row of the seats, watching me.

He walked down to me and put his hand out. When I

reached to shake it, glad for some measure of comfort, he shook his head impatiently. "No, give me the keys to the car," he said. "You won't be needing it."

I found the truck in a far corner of the parking lot, ignition key in the ashtray as usual. I dawdled, preferring not to get home so quickly as to hear his happy recounting of the night to my mother, so it wasn't until much later that I learned that he'd been the one who'd encountered Ma and Pa Burritt in town and reminded them of the details of my background.

■

There were others, of course: a couple of girls in college; a waitress in Barrington; a fellow reporter at the *Chronicle* who had graduated from Wellesley and come South because it would annoy her parents; another fellow reporter who would insist on honest opinions about her work and then cry when she got them; a newly divorced bank teller who spent four months pushing my hand away from her secret spots and telling me she was still healing from her marriage before eloping with the security guard in the lobby; and a happily promiscuous billing clerk at the Barrington water department who would whisper astonishingly explicit requests in my ear in her choirgirl's voice, leaving me no time to wonder where she'd learned one thing before she was suggesting another.

But none of them were Jocelyn, or were even a little like her. It was as if the single best quality of every woman I'd ever known—the virtue of one, the ardor of another, the courage, intelligence and humor of yet others—had been rolled into one vital package and dropped onto the beach beside me. And best of all, she accepted my quirks and deficiencies with a remarkable equanimity, which left me relaxed and confident where I had always previously been anxious and uncertain. It was almost as if she already knew me.

I'd never felt as if I had much going for me aside from the

ability to stack words this way and that; it was my solace when all else fell into ruin, the one place where I exercised mastery and certitude. But it had counted for nothing with Jocelyn at first. So that, of course, was to become my gift to her. She had valued in me the things that I had long believed turned other people away. In return, I would do for her what I did best.

CHAPTER NINE

Let me tell you about my home.

Like most homes, it's pretty undistinguished. I have a living room where I do my living. I have a bathroom where I do my bathing. I have a bedroom where I . . . well, sleep, mostly. And I have a kitchen where I eat.

I have a few things hung on the wall here and there, none of them particularly nice and certainly none of them expensive. Books and magazines are scattered about in piles. I try to keep clothes hung and dishes washed, but my attention is inconsistent. My home is a bit of a mess, actually.

Here's a true story: I lost a sandwich there once. I had just prepared it one afternoon when the phone rang, so I set it down somewhere while I talked. It was a long call from the office, and several times I had to paw through papers and move some piles around. When the call ended, I sort of forgot about the sandwich. I watched television awhile, then went out for the evening. I didn't remember it until the next day. I looked around for it, but never found it. It's still in my home. Somewhere.

I've lived here a year and have grown quite comfortable. Mr. Potkin down the hall is also comfortable. He's been here 18 years. And Mrs. Edelman on the second floor has grown quite comfortable in her 23 years here, even though she's been alone in her apartment ever since her husband dropped dead on the second day of their retirement. She's our resident historian, although she tends to treat history as a collection of great secrets to be shared only with a few hundred friends, delivery people, tourists, mail carriers or anyone else who wanders by.

"You see that pay phone there?" Mrs. Edelman whispered to me on my first stroll through the lobby after moving in. "Meyer Lansky made calls from that phone all the time. Said people listened in when he called from home. Mr. Big Shot Gangster didn't have change one time, had to borrow a dime from me. He sent me flowers."

We like where we live. Mr. Potkin, Mrs. Edelman and I are all settled and happy.

So why does Laney Pritchard want to destroy our home?

Pritchard, the soon-to-be owner of my home, is a developer. That in itself is a partial answer: Although developers see themselves as builders of monuments, people who give us the structures that span and unite the generations, their jobs necessarily require that they destroy something first. Sometimes it means tearing down places like my home. Sometimes it means paving over the marshes and fields built by the biggest developer of them all.

But beyond that, the question seems unanswerable. My home is a classic Art Deco building, with 21 apartments divided between three floors. It was built during Miami Beach's heyday and has survived a couple of hurricanes, decades of sun and salt air, and a bad paint job. A few years back, one of its owners invested money in a few repairs and some tasteful colors, and the building responded well. It now has the sort of dignity one sees in former Hollywood starlets who age well and actually learn how to act. Architectural Digest has featured my home in its pages. Preservationists want to make it part of what they hope will become a protected Art Deco district. It is being described with a word that makes developers cringe: "treasure."

Even architectural treasures can lose money, however. But my building is fully rented to decent, God-fearing people (except for Mr. Morris on the third floor, who wanted me to say that he may be 77 years old, but he's better than decent). We all pay in full every month. There are no structural deficiencies to siphon off money. In other words, it doesn't make sense to tear my building down—unless you pay an outlandish price for it and have to tear it down so you can build something people will pay a lot more for.

Here's the problem: Pritchard apparently has agreed to pay an outlandish price.

I called to ask him what his intentions were for my building. I hoped we could have a fine talk about the value of old buildings and old people. But Pritchard was having none of that. "I've got nothing to say to any of you maggots at the Post-Star," he said after I introduced myself. He then hung up.

So I called other real estate people. I won't bore you with their explanations of debt service, capitalization rates and other terms that developers typically utter among themselves. But they all agreed that the situation can be reduced to one simple economic precept: My building will never generate enough money to justify the price Pritchard is paying for it.

So we'll see. Pritchard has a contract to buy my home and will take possession as soon as the financing is worked out. Only one person knows for sure what will happen, and he doesn't talk to maggots like me. But someone else—who has known Pritchard for years, has seen how he operates—has no doubt about his plans.

"That building will be rubble within days."

"Am I a source now?" Jocelyn asked. We were in bed together on a Sunday morning, with sections of the newspaper scattered about the sheets. She'd just finished reading about my home.

"You sure are," I said. "And I appreciate your help with the column too."

She twisted the section she was holding and hit me with it. "Enjoy it while you can, pal."

She then became serious. "He's going to find out, you know."

■

We talked about my mother often. We talked of her husband too. It was what we shared: lives defined by others. I was a man who so loathed my mother's helplessness that the very echo of it in another woman's voice as she asked for help had caused to me turn away. Jocelyn was a woman who had been brutalized by someone who first claimed to love her, then turned on her when she fled, alleging she was a thief and a deceiver.

And we were both aware. I knew now that my hardness did not make me a superior creature. I could keep it and focus it, use it to drill mercilessly into the deserving when warranted. But I also could cup the weak in my hands and protect them without becoming weak myself. She knew things, too. She knew she couldn't allow herself to sink into victimhood, to stand by helplessly while her husband marshaled his resources to crush her. She had to fight with what she had, and what she had was me.

Even so, she loaded the weapon gingerly.

"I could tell you so much," she said one night.

"Well, don't," I said. "It's no fun if it's easy."

We were at one of the outdoor bars on Ocean Drive that had once been an accessory to, but now supported, the aging hotels that lined the street. The two dozen poolside tables were filled and a hundred more people stood, their voices in several languages competing with the music that poured from loudspeakers and was orchestrated by a young man perched before a bank of electronic equipment on a second-floor balcony. A banner with the name of his radio station hung beneath him; we'd stumbled into some sort of event and had found a table only by a happy accident of timing, walking in at the precise moment a couple rose to leave.

Jocelyn's smell was still on me. We had reversed the usual order of lovers' nighttimes and were only now going out, and in my imagination I could see the others around us raising their noses animal-like as they caught the scent.

"Figure it out yourself, then," she said.

"I'm kidding. Tell me," I said, but the moment had passed.

A waitress making her haphazard way through the crowd finally took our drink orders, then was swallowed again as she headed for a bar in the corner. I figured the odds were no better than even that we'd see her again.

"I need to find the bathroom," Jocelyn said. "I'll bet the line's a mile long."

"Use the men's," I offered helpfully.

She shook her head. "A hundred guys all missing the same toilet? I don't think so."

I watched people watch her as she walked away. No single part was remarkable, but the whole of her somehow demanded attention. Men's appraisals were long and frank, women's cool but studied, and I often saw in both a barely perceptible reaction—a straightening of the back, a sinuous crossing of the legs—as they unconsciously sought to be her match. Several sets of eyes locked on her as she passed, one of them intensely so.

He was a bulky man in his forties, sitting at one of the far tables with a woman and another man. Jocelyn walked within ten feet of him, taking no note, but he watched her carefully as she passed, tuning out whatever conversation was being had at the table. Even at my distance I could see the other man lean forward and say the watcher's name two times, wave a hand in front of his eyes to confirm the apparent momentary hypnosis, then lean back and utter something to the woman, who laughed in response. The man ignored them both, monitoring Jocelyn until she entered the building, then turned his head back to the crowd to see if he could tell who she had been sitting with. His gaze went over me without stopping. Perhaps he expected his wife to have better taste.

There must have been almost no line. Jocelyn came out after only a minute or so and saw him right away, which stopped her in her steps. Both of us watched her carefully, and for the same reason: to see if she would look my way.

She didn't. She went straight to his table and, with fists on her hips, said something, her face sharp and unfriendly. He replied, seeming bemused, then introduced his companions, both of whom nodded politely. Jocelyn ignored them, instead saying something else to him. His reply included an expansive sweep of his hand that took in every member of the poolside crowd, and it prompted her to pick a drink off the table and throw it in his face. She then turned and left, heading not for our table but for the street.

She was being careful not to let him make a connection between us, so I waited until she was out of sight before I got up and circled around to his table, coming at him from the direction of the hotel lobby. I reached out to shake his hand as I approached.

"Laney Pritchard?" I said as we shook.

"That's right. Who are you?"

"Tad Beckman," I said.

"The writer?" he asked, looking annoyed.

I nodded. "The maggot."

"The world's got real problems, you know. Why don't you write about them?"

"You're a problem for a lot of people," I said. "But you know what? I'm the solution."

He pushed his chair back slowly and stood with deliberate menace. He had enormous wrists and hands, and although much of his bulk was surrendering to gravity, he was still impressively wide through the shoulders and chest. The perverse projectionist in my head flashed a quick clip of a movie showing Jocelyn being slapped by those hands.

"No, you're just an asshole," he said. The couple at the table didn't move.

Just then, a waitress arrived and put a fresh drink in front of him. Our drinks had never appeared, but I was willing to bet his came unbidden. I wasn't sure what I had meant to accomplish with this meeting and it seemed to be heading for only one end: He was a practiced brawler, at least with women, and stood ready for my answer to his insult.

But the arrival of his drink was my chance to break off the confrontation without seeming to retreat.

"You might want to bring him a straw," I said to the waitress. "He seems to be having trouble hitting his mouth."

I left him standing there. I found Jocelyn halfway down the block, sitting on the steps of an adjoining hotel. As I sat next to her, I could see she'd been crying.

"What did he say?" I asked.

She just shook her head. "You went to talk to him, didn't you?" she said.

"Sure did."

"Why?"

"I was counting coup, I suppose," I said.

She shook her head again, puzzled. "It's an old Indian term," I explained. "It means you have touched your enemy. A great warrior is one who has counted many coups."

She stood suddenly as if she'd just decided something, then tugged at my hand until I stood as well. "C'mon, let's go home. I need to show you something," she said.

We hadn't made her bed before we'd left just an hour before, and she primly smoothed the spread over the pillows before reaching underneath and pulling out a small suitcase. She opened it and pawed through a jumble of papers before finding a folder and handing it to me.

"I grabbed a bunch of his files before I left," she said. "I hoped there would be something I could use against him. I found this yesterday."

It took me the rest of the evening and much of the next day to make sense of the papers. But when I was done, I had him.

■

Why does she turn away from me sometimes? Why do I look up from some task, or from a magazine or book, and find her staring at me? And why do I sense uncertainty in her body? Her loyalty to him died long ago. I know that, because when I explain to her what the papers say, there is a primitive hardness in her eyes, a look of such unalloyed anticipation that even my gut tightens a bit. We are close. So very close.

■

Even as the weapon was being trained, there was something else to tend to. After a thirty-minute wade through a pile of bureaucratic forms and visits to two offices, and after being led through a bewildering maze of corridors and locked exits, I found myself in front of an anonymous door with a grate set at eye level. Through it I could see her sitting on the edge of the bed, gazing out the room window. The view was dominated by an adjoining brick building and the rusted water tower atop it.

The attendant stood beside me expectantly. I waited for a moment until it became clear he intended to go into the room with me. "Thanks. I won't be long," I said, hoping the hint was enough.

He nodded and padded toward the end of the hall to a desk, which was nestled into an alcove and protected by heavy wire. Using a key attached to his belt with a chain, he unlocked the door to the cage and stepped in, shutting the door behind him. "Let me know when you're ready to leave," he called when he'd settled behind the desk.

I watched her through the window for a minute before going in. I expected that I would find her doing the things that disturbed people are supposed to do: rocking back and forth, talking to herself, flailing at imaginary beasts that come at her from the mists. But she was serene, sitting calmly and fidgeting no more than would be expected of anyone alone in a featureless room with nothing to do.

She turned as I came in, knocking on the door while opening it.

"Hey there," I said.

"Hey, sugar," she replied.

I sat down on the bed and hugged her. She was dressed in a hospital-issue gown, but still I somehow caught the odor of the musty sweaters I'd smelled so often as a child, the layers of un-laundered clothes piled one atop another as if they were armor.

"Sorry you missed the funeral," I said.

"I wouldn't have wanted to go anyway."

"Lots of people were there," I lied. In fact, the church had been barely half-full and it was apparent to all that the minister—a baby-faced newcomer recruited from one of the region's second-tier Bible colleges—was painfully unaware of my grandfather's life.

"That's nice," she said.

"So how are you doing?"

"As good as can be expected, I guess. How 'bout you?"

"Things are fine," I said.

"How do you like Miami?"

"It's great. You should come visit."

"Yeah, maybe," she said, but her eyes had widened with alarm.

I patted her on the knee. "I'm going to see about getting you out of here."

Her alarm became panic. "No, not yet. I'm not ready." She had clutched the hem of her gown and begun wringing it into knots. "I'd prefer to wait until I feel a bit better."

"You like it here?" I said. My words sounded abrupt and rude.

"I like places where people don't steal babies at night."

"Oh, Jesus," I said, hugging her again. "No one stole your baby. I'm right here. I just grew up and moved away."

She patted my back, as if I were the distressed one and she the comforter.

"You're not the only baby in the world, you know," she said, pulling away and looking into my face. Her madness had become a perfect opacity in her eyes, and it broke my heart.

CHAPTER TEN

I've never enjoyed being wrong as much as I do now.

I was wrong recently when I said Laney Pritchard planned to tear down my apartment building. Pritchard, a developer, has a contract to buy the property and it seemed clear that the only way he could make a profit on the deal was to destroy my building and put up a new one. That's a shame, because it's a fine old building, and because lots of elderly people have lived there a long time and it's their home.

But I was wrong. It's not because my calculations were flawed; they were sound. And it's not because the people who know him misled me. They, too, are surprised by this new turn of events.

No, I was wrong because I assumed Pritchard is merely greedy and soulless. He's more than that: He's a thief.

That's where I made my mistake. I gave him credit for working within the boundaries of the law. But Pritchard's not going to tear down my building at all, because he's found a way to make a ton of money by letting it stand. He's going to use it instead to defraud a bunch of bondholders.

The explanation of how this will work is complicated, so you'll have to concentrate for a moment. But then, people like Pritchard want it to be complicated—it's their camouflage.

Here's how it works: Pritchard Development Corp. signed a

contract eight months ago to buy my apartment building, agreeing to pay $1.2 million. As with most real estate transactions, the deal will be called off if Pritchard can't get a loan to cover the purchase price. Every homebuyer has this same escape clause when they sign for a house. After all, you can't force someone to buy a property when they have no money.

But unlike a homebuyer, Pritchard hasn't stopped by his local bank to see a loan officer. Bankers, who are captive to the notion that people should repay loans, tend to be picky about who they give money to. They ask you to prove that you're decent, upstanding and honorable. Little wonder Pritchard avoided them.

And Pritchard certainly wasn't going to pay for the building himself. That runs contrary to the developer's credo: Use Other People's Money. You never, ever put your own fortune at risk.

So Pritchard decided he would sell bonds and use the proceeds to buy the building. This is where it gets tricky.

There are a couple of things to remember about bonds. First, the people who buy bonds are as conservative as bankers. That's why they like bonds. While stocks can fluctuate wildly and even lose value, a bond has a guaranteed rate of return. It's true that a bond trader can get squashed when interest rates shift, but if you're buying bonds to hold—not trade—you're usually fine.

Second, bond buyers like to buy from established, known, recognizable entities: big corporations, the U.S. Treasury, city and state governments. They don't buy bonds from shifty guys in South Florida. So Pritchard needed someone to issue bonds on his behalf and give him the money. But who would do that?

Let me introduce you to the Miami Beach Housing Development Authority.

The authority, which was established 19 years ago, is a low-profile bureaucracy which inhabits a small office in the corner of city hall and only has contact with the public when someone gets lost on their way to the driver's license bureau and wan-

ders in accidentally. The authority has a five-person board, a staff attorney, three administrative assistants, two photocopying machines and a 317-word mission statement framed on the wall. Boiled down to its essence, here's what that statement says: Money available here, only a few questions asked.

Actually, the authority does only one thing: It puts its name on bonds. When a guy like Pritchard comes in and says he'd like to create housing for the poor or the elderly, the authority has him fill out a few forms, checks his calculations to make sure the project seems financially feasible, then issues the bonds and gives him the money. In theory, it's a no-risk proposition. A needed bit of housing gets built and the developer—not the city—is on the hook to pay off the bonds. If the project goes belly-up, it's the bond buyers' tough luck.

But why should bond buyers worry? After all, those bonds are from the Miami Beach Housing Development Authority, which has never seen one of its issues default.

They should worry because Pritchard has cooked the books.

You see, even though Pritchard is buying my apartment building, he's not the one asking for the bonds. That request is coming from something called Island Development Corp., which has hired Pritchard to act as its go-between with the authority. Pritchard explained to the authority that Island Development will buy the building from him after he's taken possession. He'll stay on as property manager, Pritchard said, but he won't own it long.

The authority didn't much care. It asked for details about Island Development and Pritchard supplied documents showing it was an investment trust based in the Netherlands Antilles. The authority then asked if Island Development was confident that it could pay off the bonds. Pritchard supplied yet more documents showing that Island Development's independent auditor had examined the financials and declared them sound.

That was that. The authority is now prepared to issue $2.3 *million in bonds and hand the money over to Island Development, which will then hand it over to Pritchard.*

But there are two things the authority doesn't know, but should: Pritchard secretly owns Island Development. And Island Development has no intention of paying off the bonds. It couldn't, even if it wished to do so. Pritchard prepared the "independent audit" himself, and its projections of revenue are pure fiction.

It's a neat trick. Pritchard spends a little more than a million dollars to get the apartment building, then sells it immediately to a bogus company for more than twice that price and pockets the difference. The bogus firm probably makes the first couple of bond payments for appearances' sake, then lets the bonds go into default and stands aside as bondholders bounce off the Byzantine corporate laws in the Netherlands Antilles before finally giving up and foreclosing on the building in hopes of getting some payoff. Any payoff. In the meantime, the building sinks into disrepair and tenants eventually move away. This is how slums are born.

Sorry, Laney. Your little shell game is over. Find somebody else to defraud.

Manzini later told the lawyers he'd never seen a column undergo more rigorous scrutiny before publication. I knew it would, so I was ready.

Still, I couldn't resist toying with Frances, the midlevel editor who'd been assigned the task of nagging me about deadlines and editing my columns. She was twitchy and obsessive, and managed to chew up huge chunks of time fussing over inconsequential matters, in the way of people who have too little to do and too much time in which to do it. She would pounce on adjectives and pronouns with a missionary's determination, demanding to know, for instance, how I had decided that a councilman with a taste for travel was a "junketeer," and suggesting that in the absence of a chain of conclusions as precise as a mathematician's proof, I had merely offered up an opinion.

"Of course it's an opinion, Frances," I would reply. "The whole column's fraught with opinions. And you know what? That's why people read it."

She would then complain to Manzini, declaring that the newspaper's integrity could be guarded only through the relentless excision of such careless judgments. But Manzini, who knew the greatest sin was to bore readers, would tell her to forget about it and send her back to her desk, where she would wait unhappily for me to deliver my next assault on her temple of neutrality. I was a hero among the rank-and-file beat reporters, because I won the battles they usually lost: My columns may have been lost to her, but Frances had better luck with the vivisections she performed on their news articles.

So that morning, I had left her a note saying only that my next column was ready, giving her no warning of its contents. When I came back from lunch with Jocelyn, I found her exactly as I knew I would: quivering and affronted, certain that my dangerous tendencies finally were on full display for all to see.

"We can't publish this," she said. "You're saying he's a criminal."

"He is a criminal," I said.

"No, he's not," she insisted. "No court has found him guilty of anything. He hasn't even been charged with anything." She was practically panting. "We can't publish this," she repeated.

"Sure we can. He's conspired to defraud people. He's planning to steal a million dollars from investors. And I can prove it."

"We can't do this. He'll sue us."

"You know, Frances, people like Laney Pritchard depend on the timidity of people like you," I said. It was cruel but true. In her world, you didn't confront evil; you argued about how to describe it while it ran loose.

"I'm telling Manzini," she said, sounding like the grade-school informer she doubtless once was.

She stalked off in search of him while I gathered the papers I knew I'd need. Jocelyn had almost immediately regretted letting me see the documents, fearful that they would prove to be trouble piled on top of trouble for her. But she'd finally come around to my way of thinking: that giving Laney something else to worry about would rob him of the energy and money that otherwise would be spent in pursuit of her. So we'd found a late-night quick-print shop and made copies of everything— letters, bond prospectus, auditor's report, and the memos labeled "private and confidential" that laid out the deal's extralegal aspects in formal and innocuous terms. Then she'd surprised me by insisting I keep the originals.

"He'll eventually notice that they're gone and he'll wonder if I have them," she explained. "Then he'll send someone over to see when I'm not home."

"He'll have someone break in?" I asked.

"He certainly will. But if they only find copies, he'll know someone else has the papers. I might need that leverage later on."

"I hadn't noticed this taste for subterfuge before," I said, not sure that I liked it.

"This is what survival looks like sometimes," she said.

I had the papers all in a stack when Manzini waved me into his office, which caused a stirring in the newsroom as my colleagues figured out that this was something beyond Frances's usual challenge. A copy of the column was on his desk, tattooed in several places by Frances's red grease pencil. She hovered next to his desk, still quivering at my effrontery, as I sat.

"Well, this would certainly be a surprise for tomorrow's readers," he began. "They're used to innuendo and insinuation. Straight talk would be a rare treat." He paused for a moment, then asked: "Is this straight talk?"

"Straight up," I said.

Frances opened her mouth to say something, but Manzini cut her off with a look.

"If we print this, it has to be absolutely bulletproof. Is it?"

I set the papers on his desk. "You'll want me to walk you through this, of course."

He nodded. "Of course."

We spent an hour pawing through the papers, with Frances having little success in her role of loyal opposition. It was a hopeless task: Manzini loved to stir the stew, and the column was one of the larger spoons he'd been handed in a while.

But I also knew he wouldn't overrule Frances on the spot. He would surely have the paper's lawyer read the column, and I suspected he would quietly assign another reporter to vet it, ordering him to check public records and incorporation documents to confirm my assertions. My only job now was to wait until Manzini found a way to get it published.

I didn't have to wait long. At the end of the afternoon, with the deadline looming for the paper's early editions to be delivered to frontier outposts like Palm Beach, we again convened in Manzini's office. Frances was there, looking beleaguered from what I suspect had been a private inspirational flogging from Manzini, as were two new members of the board of inquisition: Quarles, a partner in the downtown law firm that handled the *Post-Star*'s legal matters; and Rabinowitz, an unctuous Ivy Leaguer who had joined the reporting staff as a summer intern the previous year and stayed on as a Doberman-in-training. I was right on both counts.

There were no preliminaries. "We all know why we're here," Manzini said. "The press starts in ninety-five minutes. Everyone's read the column. Beckman proposes to tell the world that a respectable member of the business community in fact has larceny in his heart. What say ye?" His eyes settled on Rabinowitz.

The rookie's instinct for the jugular was still unrefined. Clearly uneasy, he began shuffling through his notebook as color crept up his neck. Rabinowitz, in the recent few moments, had figured out his position was untenable: He was caught between two newsroom forces whose influence hit him at distinctly different levels. Frances routinely handled his copy and could ensure that he died of a thousand cuts as she picked over each sentence, keeping him late into the night in word-to-word combat as his fellow pups gathered somewhere to drink and boast of the meat they had that day devoured. While I had no supervision over him, I could do something much worse. I could tell the world he was dickless.

And as he knew, a Doberman without a dick is no Doberman at all. "It looks fine to me," he finally said.

Manzini pounced. "What do you mean it looks fine?"

"I mean everything seems to check out."

"Jesus, do I have to drag the details out of you? Did you go to the housing authority?"

"Yes," Rabinowitz said.

"Is there a file with Laney Pritchard's name on it?"

"Yes. Well, no, not exactly. There's an application for financing from a company called Island Development and Pritchard's fingerprints are all over it."

"Meaning what, exactly?"

"Meaning he filed the application on behalf of Island Development. And meaning there's a copy of a sales contract that identifies him as the buyer of the apartment building that Island Development itself wants to buy."

"Anything else?" Manzini said.

"Well, like Tad says, there's a consultant's report that says the building can throw off enough cash to cover bond payments once certain improvements are made. And there's a recommendation from the agency staff that the bond issue be approved."

"What else?" Manzini said again.

Rabinowitz hesitated. "He was there," he said after a moment.

"Who?"

"Pritchard. He came in while I was there. They'd brought the file out front, so I had it all spread out on the counter. The lady behind the counter asked if she could help him, but he'd already spotted me. He got pretty hot."

Something stirred deep in my mind, then was gone.

"What did he say?" Manzini said.

"He wanted to know who I was and what I was doing."

"What did you say?"

"I told him these were all public documents and I goddamn well didn't have to explain myself to anyone," Rabinowitz said. Manzini nodded approvingly. "But he figured it out. He asked me if I was carrying water for Beckman. Then he asked me if this was how people made the varsity squad at the *Post-Star*. He was really quite loud and nasty about it."

Rabinowitz, working hard at sounding injured, paused for a moment, then added: "He said to tell you we're wrong."

"Tell who?" Manzini said.

"He didn't say exactly. He just said, 'Tell them they're wrong about me. You people have this whole thing wrong.' It was kind of weird, considering how Tad's column begins."

Rabinowitz hesitated again, as if deciding whether to add a last thought. Manzini, uncharacteristically patient, waited him out.

"Then he left. I don't know why he was even there. Maybe he had something to do, but after that big scene maybe he thought it was better to just leave." Rabinowitz finally came around to his point. "He said one last thing, though. He told me to ask you"—his gaze swiveled to me—"if you thought the Pulitzer people might settle for just having a career ruined for no reason. Or did he have to die like that woman did?"

I felt the blood in my face. It was personal now.

■

"Good boy," Manzini said a few moments later as he dismissed Rabinowitz. He forgot, however, to scratch him behind the ears.

Then it was Quarles's turn, and as he waited for Manzini's prompt he occupied himself with his clothes: tugging at his shirt cuffs, flicking a bit of lint from his trousers, and fingering the knot of his tie with the care and delicacy of a new lover. His patience was palpable. It was the kind of calm one acquires when almost every daylight moment—even the idle time spent waiting to be asked for an opinion—is billed at hundreds of dollars an hour.

"Well, Counselor, what do you make of this?" Manzini asked after the door closed behind Rabinowitz.

Quarles, who already had affixed a grave look to his face, pursed his lips for a second, then rumbled his answer. "There are, of course, certain things knowable from the public documents and reasonable conclusions to be drawn from them. We know Mr. Pritchard has a contract to buy the property at one price and that the other company, this Island Development, intends to buy it from him at another price. And we know that Island Development intends to finance the purchase with the bond issue that Mr. Pritchard has arranged. That in and of itself suggests a certain conflict of interest."

Manzini interrupted him. "I know what the goddamn city records say. I've got a hundred reporters who can tell me that without charging me to sit in my office while they do it."

Quarles was unperturbed. "Indeed you do. Now, then. There are three soft parts in the column. First is Tad's assertion that Pritchard is in fact the owner of Island Development. We might as well start there."

Manzini looked at me. "You're up," he said.

For the second time that afternoon, I shuffled through the papers and spread them on Manzini's desk. My presentation had gotten better with practice, becoming as seamless as a prosecutor's closing argument. The papers were damning: Among them were a letter from a solicitor in the Netherlands Antilles notifying Pritchard that Island Development was now a legally incorporated trust, along with his bill for setting it up; a second letter from the solicitor, its tone a little embarrassed, saying that he'd neglected to mention that Pritchard needed to pay Island Development's annual taxes; and a copy of a note from Pritchard to the solicitor, a handwritten scribble that had apparently been attached to some other document. It said: "Here's what the audit needs to say. Housing Authority needs by Aug. 29. That's three weeks. Chop chop."

Quarles was a good listener, quiet but clearly skeptical. When I was done, he collected the papers on the desk, took custody of the file folder with the remaining papers and assembled them together. He then rearranged them in some private fashion, stopping occasionally to ponder one before flipping back to refer to a previous page. As he worked, I gazed through the glass wall of Manzini's office, watching as knots of reporters formed and then dissolved while they talked about the column and surreptitiously monitored what was going on inside. They'd all read the column, of course, plundering through the computer system until they'd found it in its pre-Frances form, and they now waited for a ruling. This was a test for Manzini, and he knew it: Generals don't inspire their troops by wringing their hands and edging away from the battlefield. The copy-desk chief approached the office and shrugged his impatience, holding his arms out and hands up. Manzini shook his head. *Wait.*

Quarles looked up from the papers in his lap. "I've been meaning to ask. Why does this have to run tomorrow?"

"Because the bond issue is scheduled to hit the market tomorrow," Manzini said. "It doesn't do any good if we come out a few days from now and say, 'Oh, by the way, those bonds you bought? They're worthless. Sorry we didn't tell you sooner.'"

"I see," Quarles said and returned his attention to the papers. A few moments later he put the file back on the desk.

"Well, this takes care of two soft spots. It's clear that Pritchard owns Island Development and it's implicitly clear that he cooked the audit. But that leaves the third one: How do you know he's planning to default on the bonds?"

"Because he doesn't say anything about it," I said.

Quarles moved so quickly through the opening that he didn't notice where it led. "That's my point," he said. "There's nothing in any of these documents that suggests he plans to default. In fact, I don't see a reference anywhere to the bond issue."

I said nothing, letting his words hang in the air. Manzini, having been walked through the papers earlier, also sat quietly and waited. Several long seconds went by.

It finally clicked. "Ah," Quarles said. "Got it."

I repeated his words for him: "No reference anywhere to the bond issue."

"Yes, of course," he said happily. "One would think there would be at least the barest discussion of an escrow account, or a payment timetable, or something, eh?" He picked the file up from the desk. "Let me make copies of everything. You've tried to call the trustee for Island Development?" It was an instruction disguised as a question.

"He wouldn't talk. The only thing he confirmed is that the company was established as an investment trust in the past year," I said.

"Your questions have exhibited a cautious, professional approach? There's nothing personal here, aside from a journalist's outrage that some bit of financial chicanery may affect his elderly, innocent neighbors?"

I knew my lines and didn't mind lying. "I'm comforting the afflicted and afflicting the comfortable."

"Afflict away," Quarles said, standing to leave. "One more thing, though. How did you come to be in possession of these documents? And how do you know they're authentic?"

"What I tell you doesn't leave this office?" I asked.

Quarles nodded.

"His wife gave them to me," I said. "They're real."

Manzini smirked. "How's that for a source?"

■

I stayed for another two hours, protecting the column from Frances's predations and hovering while a copy editor fussed over a headline. Manzini disappeared for a while, then suddenly was at my elbow in the newsroom, holding a copy of the column and laughing.

"I took it upstairs to the old man so he could read it," he said, referring to the *Post-Star*'s publisher. "It's best that he not be surprised in the morning."

"How'd he take it?" I asked.

"Well, after we got him revived, he insisted we call Quarles again. We're solid with this. After he left here, Quarles talked to one of his partners, a guy who does securities work. That guy says, yeah, there has to be some formal mechanism to get money to the bondholders. In fact, he says he doesn't think any reputable brokerage would even touch this. The prospectus is a mess. In any event, he says we probably should report this to the Securities and Exchange Commission."

"We will," I said. "In fact, we'll print up a few hundred thousand notices and spread them all over town."

"Indeed we will," Manzini said.

■

I tried calling Jocelyn several times during the evening. I had one clean, clear victory within reach, and I wanted her to hear the details. I didn't expect her gratitude nor even want it, particularly. What I wanted was for her to be someone else for a moment, wanted the chance to pretend that she had asked me for help and that I had delivered it, swiftly and fearlessly. Then I wanted her to understand that she could now begin thinking about what was ahead. For us.

She never answered the phone.

CHAPTER ELEVEN

In many ways, the heart is ahead of the mind. When something inconsistent and elusive enters our lives, the heart will accept it readily while the mind continues to grind away logically, trapped by its inability to acknowledge the things it cannot see. The heart holds its knowledge confidently and quietly while the mind becomes frayed and overheated as it seeks to process flawed and irreconcilable bits of information. It is in those moments that the extremes of emotion are born: madness, vengeance, suicide and murder. Occasionally, however, the heart steps in and pulls the curtain back on knowledge, awarding the mind a moment of absolute clarity.

My phone calls went unanswered through the night. I did not sleep as my awareness grew. Shortly before dawn, when it was too late—long after the mammoth printing presses had rumbled to life and given birth to my last column—my heart took mercy and drew back the curtain, letting me see the fragment of Rabinowitz's tale that made everything fall into place.

■

My own phone rang several times during the morning. I knew who it was and who it wasn't: Manzini wanted me desperately and Jocelyn had no further need of me. I ignored it as I showered and ate breakfast, more out of habit than hunger. I would offer myself up to Manzini soon enough.

I drove along the causeway toward downtown, past a pair of cruise ships moored at the port. The sight of them dredged up the memory of a story I once heard from a young woman who had worked for a short time on a cruise ship. I had asked her what it was like. I wasn't so naive as to think it was a happy romp on the high seas; instead, I was curious to know how wide was the gulf that separated the bucolic life portrayed in advertising and the reality of life aboard ship.

"The problem is that there is no gulf," she replied. "The ships are perfect little microcosms of the world. The top officers are these cold-eyed Aryans, usually from places like Sweden or Norway. Others of them are Greeks. But they all have this sailing gene bred into them. They are utterly confident and arrogant. The other officers are all happy and handsome and white, and if you stop any one of them and ask for something they do it"—she snapped her finger—"like that. Passengers can't believe it. There are not too many places left where customers are pampered like that.

"But if you're alert, you'll notice pretty quickly that the real work is being done by little brown people. And if you watch them closely, you'll see that they're not all that happy. They live in fear. One spilled dish in the dining room, one complaint from someone who didn't like the way a bed was made, they're back belowdecks.

"Now, there's a place every cruise-ship passenger should see. Do you have any idea how many people work out of sight on those ships? Running the laundry, preparing the food, maintaining the engines and things? It's hundreds. Some of them never see daylight during the whole trip. You think the cruise line is going to let them mingle with passengers? Pop up to the sun deck for a quick cigarette during break time? No way. I had to go belowdecks once on an errand, and it was like visiting another country. I saw a whole family squatted down around an open fire they'd lit in a big bucket, all eating out of one dish. I felt like I had wandered into an alley in the poorest part of Calcutta.

"So, yeah, it's fantasy. But it's fantasy that depends on a willful blindness to reality."

But then, what fantasy doesn't require a blind eye?

■

Emile gave nothing away. His desk was the moat before the castle and he was the keeper of the drawbridge. All visitors— aggrieved readers, unhappy news sources, delivery people, destitute advertisers clutching past-due notices, mourning mothers with photos of newly dead children in one hand and obituary forms in the other, politicians currying goodwill from editorial writers—were required to confront Emile's expressionless, anthracite eyes and state their business. If trouble indeed did await me, it would have registered at Emile's desk first.

I got no hint that it had as I crossed the lobby. He looked up only briefly from his desk, then returned to the paperwork organized into purposeful piles before him, giving me a moment of happy doubt as I wondered if I'd spent the night agonizing over an imaginary disaster. Perhaps I'd assumed too much about Rabinowitz's testimony. Perhaps I'd let my mind wander as Jocelyn told me about her plans for an overnight visit with an old girlfriend. I would go upstairs and the Dobermans would lick my hand, maybe even curl up on the floor next to my desk and dream of the day when they, too, could be let loose on liars and thieves.

But as I walked by his desk, Emile raised his head again. "Mr. Manzini says for you to check in with him right away, please."

I stopped. "Oh?" I said, giving him a chance to elaborate.

There was a long moment of silence while we regarded each other. He was a puzzle to me. I'd noticed that his greeting each morning was precisely calibrated to match my own. When I nodded, he nodded; when I waved, he waved; my cheery "hello" was always returned, although only after being stripped of any sense of cheerfulness; and if I ignored him, he said nothing, keeping his attention focused on his desk and making mysterious notes in the visitors logbook. Once, early on, I had tried to start a conversation by asking him about some issue of the moment, but he had known instinctively that my effort was either insincere or lazy: I wasn't really interested in being his pal, and if I had hoped to take some true measure of public sentiment on the issue, then I was hilariously inept to think I could do it in the *Post-Star*'s lobby. He had dismissed me by saying curtly that he hadn't thought much about it. Sir.

This time, however, Emile softened. "Some people are here. They do not seem to be very happy."

I took the back stairs to the newsroom, which allowed me to get to my desk without having to cross the newsroom's expanse and gave me an oblique view of Manzini's glass-walled office.

Laney Pritchard was there, sitting with another man in front of Manzini's empty desk, both of them ignoring the cups of coffee that I suspected had arrived unbidden and were there only because their preparation put a cloak of good manners over a bid for time. They carried looks of injured patience.

"Where the hell have you been?" Manzini asked, suddenly at my shoulder. There was a brawler's happiness in his voice. "I thought I'd have to start the fun without you."

I ignored the question. "Have you talked to them yet?"

"Nah. His lawyer called first thing, said there were serious problems with the column. Wouldn't tell me on the phone. Said they wanted to come over."

"I thought of something last night," I said.

Manzini's radar was good. "What?" he said, his insouciance gone.

"Something Rabinowitz told us. He said that when Pritchard arrived at the housing authority office yesterday, the clerk asked if she could help him."

"Yeah, so?"

"These bond issues require a lot of paperwork. He had to be in and out of there all the time. You'd expect him to be greeted by name, but he got treated like a stranger."

Manzini mulled this for a moment. "Maybe the clerk just didn't know him. Or she was new or something."

I shook my head. "It's not that big an office. Everybody knows everybody else. Maybe she was new, but I doubt it."

"Don't worry about it," he said. "We've got documents he signed and letters he wrote. We'll give him the obligatory hour for evasions and denials, then I'll buy you lunch."

A free meal is the time-honored way for editors to pat their reporters on the head. It was supposed to make me feel better. It didn't.

■

Under Manzini's rules of engagement, only he and I were to attend the meeting. Quarles's presence would be a tacit acknowledgment that our position was legally vulnerable, giving the enemy confidence; likewise, having Frances, Rabinowitz and all other culpable parties gather in the office would have the flavor of reinforcing a questionable position with sheer numbers. So it was two of us against two of them.

Manzini's demeanor was deliberately casual. "Interesting morning, gentlemen," he said as he settled behind his desk. I sat on a couch perpendicular to the desk, with all combatants in profile. "I'm not surprised that you want to talk. So talk."

The introductions had been brief and the handshakes perfunctory. The lawyer had an Eastern European name, complicated and riddled with diphthongs, which Manzini mangled a couple of times before giving up and waving them back to their seats. His abrupt instruction to speak their business caught the lawyer by surprise.

"Do you not have any idea why we're here?" he asked.

"I know perfectly well why you're here," Manzini said. "People like Mr. Pritchard usually show up demanding the right to tell their side of the story. And it's always after they've declined other chances to do so before we've printed anything." He shifted his look to Pritchard: "We're certainly interested in hearing from you now, of course. For the record and for publication."

The lawyer had regained his equanimity. "Please direct your comments to me, sir. Mr. Pritchard will indeed respond, eventually. But let's return to the original question. Do you know why we're here?"

"I thought I just answered that."

"I suppose you did, in a way. But you're wrong. Mr. Pritchard isn't here to offer his side of the story. He has nothing to explain. There is no story, despite Mr. Beckman's claims to the contrary in his—" he hesitated for a moment, as if he couldn't find the proper word for something so vile "—writings. You, on the other hand, have much to explain."

"Such as?" Manzini asked.

"Such as how an allegedly responsible newspaper comes to publish utter fiction."

"What are you talking about? I expect you to come in here and whine about some of the details, but don't pretend like it's not true. We've got the guy's own documents, for Christ's sake."

"Yes, the documents. We're most interested in them. Please make sure you keep them secure." I could see Manzini's confusion build. "Now, then. I want to tell you something. I will say this as clearly as I can, because you people seem to have trouble getting things straight. We are suing you, Mr. Manzini. For libel. You may be able to limit the damage by printing a full retraction in tomorrow's edition. We, of course, insist on it. And you may consider some disciplinary action against your writer. Juries like that sort of thing." The lawyer allowed himself a smug moment. "That's just a bit of free advice."

Despite his uncertainty, Manzini was unwilling to believe it wasn't bluster. "Have at it, although I still don't understand how you'll deny what the documents say."

"As I said, sir, they're utter fiction. What part of that phrase confuses you? There is no bond issue. There is no application for financing at the housing authority. There is no audit. There is no Island Development, or if there is, Mr. Pritchard certainly has no connection to it." The lawyer paused, as if inviting rebuttal; when none came, he continued. "And now, there is no possibility that Mr. Pritchard will be able to buy the apartment building that has become the focus of your corrupt crusade. Mr. Pritchard's lender called him this morning to tell him that in light of today's report, his credit line has been canceled. He is now essentially bankrupt."

He paused again. I watched Pritchard closely, but his face was carefully neutral. At the same time, I could feel Manzini's eyes on me.

The lawyer finished his summary. "And that, gentlemen, is real, tangible and measurable economic damage."

Manzini had one more card to play, and he used it. "We'll obviously investigate all this. But you know what? When you sue us, everything's up for grabs. If Mr. Pritchard thinks his reputation has been stained, then his reputation has to withstand scrutiny. And I'm afraid Mr. Pritchard has a reputation as a wife beater."

Pritchard, who had been silent until this point, delivered the coup de grâce himself.

"What are you talking about? I've never been married."

■

It got worse.

The housing authority's executive director lodged his own complaint later that same day. There was indeed no bond issue pending, he confirmed. Some weeks prior, Pritchard had requested the appropriate paperwork to apply for bond financing, but after completing and returning the documents, he'd asked the authority simply to hold the application for the moment; his purchase of the property was still pending, he'd explained, and he didn't have the legal standing to apply for financing on behalf of Island Development.

Curious thing, though, the director added: After reading the column that morning, and taking care to know exactly what was in the file so that his outrage could be calibrated accordingly, he'd had his secretary retrieve it.

"Someone"—he cocked an eyebrow at Manzini and me to let us know the *Post-Star* harbored his leading suspect—"has inserted a completely fraudulent set of papers in that file. There's a fictitious letter from someone who purports to be a staff analyst and some mumbo jumbo about an approval. Honestly. The whole thing's absurd. It would never happen that quickly." Bureaucratic efficiency, it seems, was an accusation, not a virtue.

"Are you suggesting that someone here planted this stuff in the file?" Manzini demanded. "Why in God's name would anyone do that?"

"I don't know," the director said testily. "But the only people my staff remembers handling the file are your reporters. Mr. Beckman here and that young fellow. It's been of no interest to anyone else."

"How about Laney Pritchard? Did he ever come in to review the file?" I asked.

The director flapped his hand dismissively, as if such bizarre questions could be waved away. "I suppose. But surely you're not saying he somehow arranged his own lynching, are you?"

■

Quarles made the same point.

"Let me set this out as if I were Pritchard's lawyer," he said. "This is the argument I would make to a jury. You tell me if I've misunderstood something."

We were in Manzini's office for the third time that day.
Quarles had spent much of the afternoon interviewing me,
Manzini and Rabinowitz, talking with us separately and taking
scrupulous notes, giving the exercise the flavor of an interrogation. He'd also consulted with Pritchard's lawyer at length,
seeking to get a precise measure of what it would take to make
them less unhappy. And at some unacknowledged point, it became clear that no one placed faith in my column any longer.
The only task before us was to negotiate the terms of surrender.

"Mr. Beckman is a columnist of noted ability, with both
readership and prizes to prove it. He is also a man with the singular ability to use words as a weapon. In most cases, he wields
this weapon to the benefit of everyone. In one case, however, he
drew his weapon to only benefit himself.

"Mr. Beckman lives happily in an apartment building that
Laney Pritchard hoped to buy. Mr. Beckman decided that Mr.
Pritchard's ownership of the building somehow posed a threat
to his happy little life, and he set out to derail that purchase.
His first column sought to stir up architectural preservationists,
but to no avail. So he wrote a second column that carried alle-
gations of trickery and criminality. That column accomplished
what the first failed to do: It killed Mr. Pritchard's deal.

"But Mr. Beckman's zeal caused him to reach too far. He
based his second column on documents that were later shown
to be false, documents that somehow were added to a file Mr.
Pritchard had opened with a municipal agency for possible future use. How these documents came to be is a mystery. Even
though Mr. Beckman has denied any culpability in their cre-
ation, he somehow knew where to find them and how to use
them to ruin Mr. Pritchard.

"Mr. Beckman was also heard to threaten Mr. Pritchard one
evening. As he sat quietly with companions at a club, Mr.
Pritchard was approached by the columnist and told that he
was a 'problem' and that Mr. Beckman saw himself as the 'solution.'"

Quarles let us absorb this as he shed his role. His last words were delivered in a dull tone: Being on the winning side, even if he was just pretending, had animated him.

"If this goes to court, Tad, you'll have to give a full recounting. Perhaps you should try it now for practice."

CHAPTER TWELVE

Where should I begin? Was I supposed to start with my earliest memories, to tell them of a childhood spent as an unwelcome visitor, the spawn of a rebellion that my mother had no will to continue? Or was it better to start by telling them what it was like to be a permanent outsider, never quite belonging to anyone or any place and aware that acceptance was always conditional? Perhaps I should have instructed them on helplessness: told them how I had loathed it for so long, then sought it out as atonement. I could have done all that. They would have understood, then, what it was like to meet Jocelyn, to find someone who didn't ask for help or comfort, but needed both and accepted both.

I told them none of it, however. It didn't matter anyway. Nothing I could have said would have disguised an elemental truth: I had been seduced and set up.

Manzini, predictably, provided the plain-English translation after I'd finished my story. "Let me see if I've got this straight. Some woman plops down next to you on the beach one afternoon, plays winky-wink with you for a while, eventually takes you to bed and then just happens to have some juicy information for you. Are you really that fatuous? I'm surprised she didn't just show you her tits and tell you to come get 'em, big boy."

"She did, actually," I said.

"Oh, Jesus," Manzini said, putting his head in his hands. "At least tell me they were marvelous."

"I tried not to look."

Manzini lifted his head. "Too bad you didn't try harder. One look seems to have done it."

Quarles cut in. "It'll help if we get a fix on what we know and what we don't know. What we know—"

Manzini interrupted him. "What we know is that my ace here saw some tits and lost his mind."

Quarles ignored him. "What we know is that this person struck up a friendship with Tad, told him a convincing story about her background, let him conclude that he could both help her out of what seemed to be a brutal relationship and perform a greater good on behalf of his elderly neighbors, then gave him cleverly doctored papers to use in his reporting." Unlike Manzini, who seemed to be focused on Jocelyn's breasts, Quarles was carefully noncarnal: Even though my "friendship" with this person had soiled many a sheet, sex was only the means, not the reason, and therefore didn't deserve to become a distraction.

"What we don't know is why. This person presumably had cause to want to hurt Laney Pritchard, and was smart enough to know how to do it. Even to the point of knowing that Tad would look for supporting evidence at the housing authority, and that it had to be there. So we need to find this person."

Both of them looked at me for a long moment. When I didn't say anything, Manzini asked, "When's the last time you saw her? Or spoke to her?"

"A couple of days ago."

"Do you know where she lives?"

"Of course."

"Do you know where she works?" he continued.

"She didn't work."

"Keeping you happy must have been a full-time job."

"Oh, shut up," I said, suddenly tired of him. "You've made your point."

"We have ten days," Quarles said.

"Why ten?" Manzini asked.

"Pritchard's lawyer filed the lawsuit today just as the court clerk was closing up. Under state statute, we have up to ten days to respond. The clock begins ticking at the start of court business tomorrow."

"We don't need to find her before we respond, do we?" Manzini said. "It's clear what we're going to say. We were set up."

Quarles nodded even as he disagreed. "That is indeed what we want to say. But you never say what you can't prove, so it would be foolish and reckless for us to claim a conspiracy when all we have is Tad's tale."

"What happens at the end of ten days if we don't find her?" Manzini asked.

"Then we start negotiations," Quarles said. "If I were Pritchard's lawyer, my opening bid would be about three million. And I'd only give you twenty-four hours before I started increasing that in half-million-dollar increments. We could, of course, tie this up for a long time. There's a big backlog in civil court and it might be years before it goes to trial. But that just means you'll pay him as much as you would now, plus what will doubtless be an enormous attorney's fee." His smile was meant to be rueful but seemed more like envy.

Manzini turned toward me. "You'd better start looking."

■

On my way through the lobby I noticed a worker changing the display boards, tacking up a new set of photographs for visitors to ponder. I recalled the first time I'd seen the display, and the memory that there was something important there taunted me again, then hid beyond my reach.

I asked Emile if I could make a call. He nodded toward a

phone on a table behind him, which had a staff directory next to it and a sign above it instructing that only in-building calls were allowed. I looked up the extension for the promotions department and dialed it.

The phone at Emile's desk rang. "Front lobby," he answered into my ear.

"I take it they're gone for the day," I said, feeling foolish for using the phone to talk to someone only steps away.

"After hours it rings here, sir," Emile confirmed. He waited, still facing away and apparently unperturbed.

"Okay, thanks," I said, hanging up.

I dialed the number for the photography department, snickering as I did at the prospect of getting Emile again. I saw the muscles in his back tense slightly and I knew he thought I was mocking him. Sure enough, his phone rang again.

"Front lobby," he said with the same inflection. He would meet my provocations with an immutable dignity.

This time I hung up without saying anything and walked to the front of his desk. "Listen, I don't mean to pester you. I should have just asked you first rather than dialing numbers willy-nilly. Who handles those photographs?" I pointed toward the display boards.

"It is the photography department," he said. "But you must use the night number after five o'clock."

He didn't offer the number, however; I suppose that was my punishment. I returned to the in-house phone and looked it up.

One of the photographers answered on the first ring.

"Yeah, they're all up here somewhere," he said after I'd asked about photos from past displays.

"Can I look at them?"

"I'll have to find them. It might take a few minutes," he said. "But I can't do it right now. I've got two assignments, so I've got to get out of here. Tell you what. Meet me in the photo lab about nine. I'll get them for you then."

"I'll be there," I said, wondering if word had trickled out to other departments.

It hadn't. "Loved the column today, by the way," he said.

■

I went home. Sitting by a window overlooking the Intracoastal Waterway, I watched the sun settle behind the tallest of Miami's office buildings, a perfect alignment that would be knocked a-kilter within days as the earth wobbled toward its next equinox. I mulled the absurdity of my task. How the devil was I supposed to find her? I was no cop. I had no power of intimidation or subpoena. I couldn't seize travel records or credit card receipts. I could ask her acquaintances about her, but I realized I knew of only a pitiful few. There was the manager of her apartment building, a woman on the same floor whom Jocelyn had seemed friendly with, and . . . well, that was all.

Idly, I picked up the phone and dialed her number again, as I had dozens of times in the past two days. This time, someone answered.

"Hello?" It was a man's voice, and the Latin accent was carried on even that single word.

"Who is this?" I asked, surprised.

"Julio." The building manager.

"Is Mrs."—suddenly I wasn't even sure what to call her—"uh, is Jocelyn there?"

"No, she is not being here," he said. Julio was a recent Cuban arrival, a *Marielito,* whose grasp of English was still evolving. His sense of maintenance was likewise rudimentary: He tended to talk to inanimate objects as he sought to repair them, usually fruitlessly. Jocelyn and I had giggled for hours one night after seeing him chatter away at a jammed door lock.

"What are you doing there?"

"I am checking for damaged."

"So she's moved away?"

"Yes, that is so," he said. Then he added: "Is this Mr. Beckman?"

"That's right," I replied.

"She told me you come and get some stuffs here. You find me, I let you in."

■

I went immediately to her building, but Julio, probably deep in conversation with a water pipe, was nowhere to be found. I climbed the two flights to Jocelyn's floor and tried her door, but it was locked. I looked up and down the corridor, trying to remember which apartment belonged to her friend, a tall black woman. I finally knocked on one across the hall and down a bit, dredging up a name as I heard someone approach the door from the other side. Myra.

"Hi," she said as she opened it. I'd seen a flicker of light from the peephole the moment before. "How are you?"

"Good, thanks. Listen, have you seen Jocelyn lately?"

She looked uncomfortable. "Well, no, not since she left the other morning. I thought you . . . ah, knew."

"That she moved away, you mean?" I said. Myra nodded. "No, it was a bit of a surprise."

"Oh. I'm sorry." She seemed to mean it.

"Do you know where she went?" I asked.

She shook her head. "Home, maybe. That's a beautiful area. I'm surprised she ever left. They haven't messed everything up there like they've done here."

"Where's that?" I said, embarrassed. I was the lover. I was supposed to know these things. Jocelyn had made a few vague references to a small town in Alabama, but had never said much and had turned aside my questions by shrugging and saying it was just an ordinary, forgettable, small-town childhood.

Also, her descriptions, infrequent as they were, had never included words like "beautiful."

"Somewhere up on the Georgia coast, I think," she said, letting surprise register on her face. "Ain't you ever heard a Geechee accent?"

"No, I haven't. And I even grew up there. Not on the coast, though."

"It wasn't very pronounced," Myra conceded. "Actually, I only heard it in a few words. But I had a boyfriend once from near Savannah, had some Geechee in him. So maybe I heard it where anyone else would have missed it."

"I just didn't catch it," I said.

"Trust me. That girl was Geechee. Even if she tried to deny it."

"She did?"

"Yeah, sort of. I asked her about it once, but she just shook her head and changed the subject. She didn't want to talk about it. In fact, she didn't talk much about anything. She was friendly, but she didn't want to be friends, you know what I mean?"

I nodded. I was finding out how true that was. "What did she do when . . ." I faltered, unsure how to ask it.

Myra finished it for me. "When the two of you weren't in there doing the wild thing?" She gave me a sly look as I nodded again. "It's all right. People do that. She didn't do anything, as far as I could tell. She was either getting ready to see you or getting back from seeing you."

"Did she ever have visitors?"

"Nah. I heard her fussing at somebody on the phone once, though. I'll bet it wasn't you. She was always real careful around you."

"What was she saying?"

"I didn't hear much. I was unlocking my door. I heard her say"—she made her voice angry, in imitation—"'Listen, you've got the easy part of this!' I didn't listen to anything else. It wasn't any of my business."

I'd run out of questions, so we regarded each other silently for a moment. "Thanks for your help," I finally said.

She nodded. "I'll tell you something," she said. "You be careful of girls that ain't got girlfriends."

■

I shouldn't have been surprised to be this late in discovering something as elemental as Jocelyn's roots. She had lived too much in the here and now for me to discover much about her past.

With Jocelyn, history always seemed like the wake of a boat: I could see the recent past immediately behind us when I bothered to look, but anything beyond that was featureless and inconsequential. She would tell me about her life with Laney and she might refer to her childhood in an offhand fashion; she also occasionally would recall a small dramatic moment or a revelatory event, the sort of thing whole people have to tell. But otherwise, she kept her face into the wind, deflecting my questions as we moved.

"Are you writing my biography?" she asked one night. I had asked for some image of her as a child: a class picture, a high school yearbook photo, something to show me what she had looked like before she became so lush and knowing. Would she also have fled in humiliation, or would she have laughed with the others, and enjoyed a boy who could temporarily join the drill team for a moment of impulsive slapstick?

"Yeah, but just the dirty parts," I said.

"It'll be a thin book."

"Well, the research isn't finished yet," I said, making a scholarly exploration of her back and thighs with my hand. "Besides, I want to know where you learned to fight like that."

"It's nothing that can be taught," she said, shifting a bit to ease my research effort.

She had struck suddenly and effectively. We'd walked earlier that evening along the boulevard which nestled against the beach, stopping at restaurants to examine the menus and handicap our chances of finding both good food and decent service in an area not known for either. We had agreed to eliminate every restaurant that carried the word "sun-dried" anywhere on its menu, which put half the places out of bounds, and the prospect of a forty-five-minute wait culled several others. We were approaching the far end of the boulevard, getting dangerously close to a corned beef sandwich, when we saw the magician.

He was a child, perhaps twelve years old, wearing a top hat and dressed in a tailcoat with sleeves rolled up and wings that almost dragged the ground. A card table with folding legs stood next to him, set with several props and an open felt-lined case holding a handful of coins and a few stray dollar bills. He was standing on the corner of the block, at the mouth of a small, unlit street that led away from the beach and seemed to exist only as a place to store garbage and empty crates between a dozen or so haphazardly parked cars. We got a hopeful look as we approached.

"Do you have a moment for amazement and wonder, sir?" he asked. "As hard as it may be to turn your attention from such beauty"—he gave a nod in Jocelyn's direction—"I can promise you'll enjoy a few moments of magic." He spoke in the hurried cadence of a youngster reciting a memorized lesson.

Jocelyn laughed and tugged at my arm. We stopped in front of his table, prompting the boy to nod and say, "I could see you were a man of distinction."

"Ah, he's just a guy with a spare dollar," Jocelyn said. "So make it good."

The boy ignored her, concentrating instead on the table. He started with a pair of interlocking rings, which he proceeded to detach with a mysterious incantation, then worked through his entire repertoire: coins taken from ears, loose handkerchiefs that somehow knotted themselves together, and the pulling from his hat of a small, ragged stuffed rabbit with one button-eye missing. When his three-minute performance was complete, he gave a deep bow, just as someone had instructed him to. We applauded, and I peeled off a dollar from the clump of bills I carried and dropped it in the case, then added another when I felt Jocelyn's elbow in my side.

"Thank you," the boy said.

"You're welcome," Jocelyn said, not hesitating to take credit for my largesse. "What's your name?"

"Stevie," he answered.

"Where did you learn this stuff?" She was friendly and re-laxed in the way of those rare adults who truly enjoy being around children. It was something I hadn't previously noticed in her, and I found it enormously attractive.

The boy, however, grew nervous at the attention. "I'm not really supposed to talk to people," he said.

"It's okay," Jocelyn said, misunderstanding him. "We'll move out of the way when someone else comes."

"He doesn't like it when I talk to people," the boy said, fix-ing his gaze on the beach over her shoulder, as if he could will her away by refusing to meet her eye.

"'He'? Who's 'he'? Who are you talking about?" Jocelyn asked.

The boy just shook his head, then looked up and down the sidewalk for his next audience. But the closest people were half a block away and had stopped in front of a store window, giv-ing Jocelyn time to bore in.

"Does somebody make you do this?"

"Not exactly. Sort of. I have to pay him for this stuff," he said, motioning to the table and props.

"Pay who?" she asked again.

"Mario. I have to pay him for rides, too. He says we're in business together."

"Do you go to school? Do you have a family?"

The boy hesitated a moment, then said, "Yes." He was clearly lying.

Suddenly there was a man standing next to us, having somehow come from the side street without being noticed. He nodded to the boy. "Stevie, howya doin'?"

"Fine," the boy said quickly.

"Pack up," the man ordered. "We need to go."

"Are you Mario?" Jocelyn said. I wondered if he caught the menace in her voice.

He ignored her, snapping the felt case shut and taking custody of it. Jocelyn stepped closer to him and spoke directly into his face. "Mario, we weren't done here. I want to see the show again."

"Show's over," the man said. He gave Stevie an I'll-deal-with-you-later look and twirled his finger in the direction of the table, but the boy didn't move. Jocelyn advanced yet another step closer, getting between the boy and the man.

"I'll bet Stevie would be glad to just stay here and have a milk shake with me," she said. "Wouldn't you, Stevie?"

The boy looked fearfully at Mario but nodded. For a second no one moved, but then Mario muttered, "This is stupid," and pushed Jocelyn away roughly and grabbed the boy's arm.

Jocelyn didn't hesitate. She drew her leg back and snapped it down on the side of Mario's knee, a combination of a kick and a stomp that bowed his leg in sickeningly and caused him to bellow in pain as he collapsed to the ground. He released his grip on the boy, and Jocelyn tugged on Stevie's sleeve until the two of them moved several feet away. Grunting through gritted teeth, the man pulled himself to the wall of the building and sat up.

"Jesus, you broke my knee, you bitch," he said, panting.

The whole incident had taken only seconds, and I felt foolish just standing there. I walked over to Mario and squatted down. "Are you related to this kid?" I asked.

"He works for me." His breath was slowing but he was still grinding his teeth together against the pain.

"Well, I think he just quit his job."

He didn't seem inclined to argue. "That stuff's mine," he said, jerking his head toward the table and magic props. "His coat's mine too."

The boy shrugged off the coat and laid it across the table. I stood to leave.

"You know, you really ought to work on your management skills," I said.

"You better hope I never catch you or your bitch girlfriend alone one night, asshole," he replied.

We walked several blocks away and found a sandwich counter, where we stopped to buy the boy a drink and question him. We then found the police substation and explained things to the two officers on duty, whose name tags identified them as Zimmerman and Robles.

After telling them what we'd learned—Stevie, it turned out, was a runaway from Homestead, where his migrant family picked vegetables in fields reclaimed from the Everglades—I added casually, "There was a little altercation too."

"Oh?" said Robles, who seemed to be in charge.

"This guy Mario got a little pushy. You know, shoving people around."

Robles grinned. "So you put him on the ground."

I felt myself color. "Well, one of us did."

He gave Jocelyn an appreciative glance, then looked over at Zimmerman. "You'd better go check it out." Turning back to us as his companion left, he said, "Hey, I'm sure you were being helpful, but you can't go around fighting with people. If this guy wants to file a complaint, you could have a long night."

But when Zimmerman returned fifteen minutes later, he just shook his head. "He's gone. He's not going to want the police involved."

A woman from the county's social services agency eventually showed up and talked with Stevie for a long time, sitting with him on a bench against the wall and patting his knee. She had a relaxed, smooth style, murmuring her questions to him and listening carefully to the answers, making it seem as if they were deciding something together. When she finally asked if he'd like to come with her, he nodded. We got a sly wink from the woman as they left, along with a wave from Stevie.

We headed back to the boulevard, keeping to the busier end where it was unlikely we'd see Mario limping into view. We were no longer hungry, though, and instead sat on the low stone wall adjacent to the beach, looking toward the water.

"I just hate this," Jocelyn said.

"Hate what?" I asked, uncertain which part of the bizarre chain of events she was referring to.

"There should be a park here," she said, sweeping her hand toward the beach and ignoring my question. "A big park, with a lawn and playground equipment and a place for families to have picnics. It should be a place where kids are safe with their mothers and fathers. No child should ever be parked on the sidewalk and made to hustle money from strangers. The only real job we've got in this world is to make things orderly and safe and calm for children. Why is that so goddamn hard for people?" She started to cry. "Why do we make children share our misery?"

I drew her close and we sat for a long minute holding each other without speaking. I pondered how to ask the question that should have occurred to me long before, wondered how to phrase it without somehow making her think there was a proper answer. I finally realized I would get no points for finesse.

"Do you have children?" I asked.

"No," she said into my chest.

Now, as I stood in the hallway in front of Myra's closed

door, with her words of warning fresh in my ear, I recalled Jocelyn's answer that night. And I remembered that despite being captivated by the thought that she would fight so ferociously on behalf of a child she didn't even know, I was sure that she was lying. I was sure she had children.

■

I found Julio in the stairwell on my way out. We trudged back up to Jocelyn's door and went in.

It was a furnished apartment, but it was obviously uninhabited. Closets and drawers were all open, being aired out, and the kitchen smelled of oven cleaner. A vacuum cleaner stood in one corner, along with a mop and pail. On a table I found a couple of my shirts, my swimsuit, a book I'd recently bought but found unreadable, and a cardboard box with an assortment of stray items inside, the sorts of things that get left in drawers, under cushions or kicked beneath furniture.

"I throw away this stuffs, so you look now, okay?" Julio said, gesturing toward the box. I nodded.

As I pawed through the detritus, I came across something I hadn't seen in years. It was a book of matches. Across the front flap was a familiar name: "Almo's Crossroads Store."

■

I was late getting to the photo lab, but the photographer himself had been delayed, so we arrived at the door at virtually the same moment. He looked at me warily. He'd heard by then.

"Does this have anything to do with the, uh, problem?" he asked.

"Maybe. I'm not sure. It's just a hunch."

He set his camera bag on a desk, took out a camera and began rewinding its film. "Let me get this started, then we'll look."

A few minutes later he led me to a small room that had started life as a supply closet but had evolved into a photo archive. File cabinets holding negatives lined one wall, while opposite them was a set of industrial-style metal shelves, where finished prints were stacked. We walked to the shelves.

"We change that display in the lobby once a month," the photographer said. "When we take down pictures we pile them up here." He pointed to a stack. "The most recent ones are on top. How long ago did you see this picture?"

"Maybe a year ago," I said.

He arbitrarily took off the top third of the stack and set it aside. "We'll start here," he said, taking the first picture from the remaining pile.

But because I couldn't describe the photo—all I had was the nagging sense that a picture, some picture, was important—he was of no help. After a while he wandered off to tend to his film, leaving me alone to paw through the stack.

I found it after twenty minutes. It was a photograph of a woman walking through what was obviously the concourse of Miami International Airport. She was dressed somberly and carried a small bag in each hand, one of which may actually have been a large purse. The picture caught her in midstride, and she seemed to be purposefully composed. But in her wake, several others in the concourse had turned to stare as she walked by, their voyeurism captured forever on film. Little wonder: Despite her attempt at composure, great tears were streaming down her face.

I took the picture to the photographer. "This is the one. Do you know who took it?"

He looked at it for only a moment before answering. "I did."

"Why was she crying?"

"I don't know. She wouldn't tell me. I was out there on another assignment when I saw her walking toward me. She wouldn't even tell me her name." He admired the photo. "This is why you keep your lens cap off. Pictures like this are a gift."

I could have told him who it was, but it wasn't important. What was memorable—what had buried itself in my memory all this time—was what Jocelyn had tucked under one arm as she marched ahead.

CHAPTER
THIRTEEN

I was waiting outside the library's main branch the next morning when the door was unlocked. I had discovered something the previous evening that rookie detectives learn on their first shift: You don't do much detecting by sitting around lamenting how little you know. One simple visit to Jocelyn's apartment had turned up two important clues—that she had visited Almo's store at some point and that she apparently was from somewhere on the Georgia coast. Then there was the photograph, which had provided not only a tangible clue but a lesson in the value of giving sway to your intuition. So I was ready to spend the morning maintaining that momentum, learning what I could about Geechee and scouring the library's bank of phone books for all references to anyone named Pritchard in the coastal settlements. In my more delirious moments, I had visions of wrapping up the whole mystery by the afternoon, dropping a detailed explanation of the conspiracy on Manzini's desk and asking casually if he still wanted a column for tomorrow as well.

But by ten o'clock, I had learned the other thing that rookie detectives eventually come to know: investigations tend to lurch.

"Nope. Can't find a thing," the man behind the information desk said after a few minutes with his computer. I'd spent a fruitless hour fingering the card catalog before finally giving up and asking a professional.

"I'm not sure of the spelling," I said. "Maybe if we tried some variations."

He took no care to hide his annoyance. "Our system accounts for that. It identifies all subjects close to that spelling and lists them. There's nothing here." He tapped a few more keys and waited. "Are you sure you don't mean Gullah? I've got several references to that."

"I'm sure." Gullah is a black dialect, an almost incomprehensible mishmash of English and African tribal tongues that evolved out of the coastal slave communities. Jocelyn was a white woman with an accent so subtle that even a neighbor with an ear for it had caught it in only a few words. I didn't mean goddamn Gullah.

"Sorry, then," he said. "The best I can do is suggest you refer to some of the textbooks on dialects. Perhaps this Geechee"— his pronunciation made clear that he doubted there really was such a thing—"is mentioned somewhere, but it's not so common that it shows up in the subject index."

My luck was no better with the phone books. Between the volumes for Savannah and Brunswick, Georgia's two largest coastal cities, there were more than a hundred listings under the name Pritchard. The book for Jacksonville, Florida—which I consulted because it's actually a Georgia city that somehow ended up on the wrong side of the state line—added another hundred or so of its own. And there were doubtless many more Pritchards in the smaller towns dotting the coast. Calling each one of them individually would eat up a great chunk of time while offering little chance of stumbling across the right person. The ten-day clock had already started to tick loudly in my head.

Besides, I could only imagine what I would say: "Is this the Pritchard residence? I'm calling from Miami and I'm looking for someone whose name might be Jocelyn, although I'm not sure. She sort of misled me on some things, you see, but anyway, I need to talk to her. She's attractive, mid-thirties, has nice bosoms, I have to say. And she's funny. She tends to come at things indirectly, so when you're around her you have to pay attention pretty much all the time. I liked being with her and I miss her terribly and I can't really believe she did this to me, so I hope that when I find her there'll be some happy explanation for all this, even though it's clear that she deceived me, which almost makes me not want to find her because I'll have to confront that, and as long as I don't find her I'm able to pretend occasionally that she really loved me. So: Have you seen her?"

That left Almo. Perhaps he could explain how Jocelyn came to have a book of matches from his store.

■

"You'd better fly," Manzini said. "It'll take too long to drive. Fly to Atlanta and rent a car. But if you're not getting anywhere, come right back."

His manner had become brusque. I could feel his fury: Given his druthers, he clearly would have preferred to flog me with a broken-off car antenna. But he needed me to protect himself. The correction had appeared in that morning's paper, a humiliating admission of error that would make all the local news broadcasts that night, but it wasn't enough. Quarles had confirmed what Laney Pritchard's lawyer had said—a correction might ease, but by no means erase, the problem. So we needed to prove that we'd been duped. My job certainly depended on it, and Manzini's job probably did too. We were two shipwreck survivors sharing a single life preserver, aware that this was not the time to debate blame or assign responsibility.

"So when are you going?" he asked.

I considered for a moment. I sensed he wanted me to leave that evening, but I had a visceral feeling that I needed to learn more about Geechee. I wanted what remained of this day to chew on it.

"I'll get the first flight tomorrow. I'll know something by noon."

It wasn't the right answer. "Oh? What, have you got a date tonight?"

"No, I just thought I'd hit the beach, maybe meet somebody." I didn't want him to feel like the only prick in the room.

Blood darkened his face. "We're really under a time crunch. Maybe I should put somebody else on it. We could cash in some credits with the police. See if she turns up anywhere in their computers."

I shrugged. "If you want. I doubt it'll do any good, though."

Manzini didn't ask why, so I didn't have to explain. I didn't have to tell him that I'd never smelled cigarette smoke in Jocelyn's hair or on her clothes, nor had I ever tasted it in her mouth. I didn't have to describe how we'd never lit a candle for love light. We'd never barbecued steaks. She didn't keep oil lamps for emergencies. There was only a single reason for her apartment to yield a book of matches, a still-perfect set that had never been tossed into the bottom of a purse or jammed into a pocket, but instead was carefully preserved to look as if it had just been lifted from the box next to Almo's cash register. It was a beacon, a lone clue she'd left behind. No one would find anything else anywhere. This was her finger crooked at me, beckoning.

■

There was again a flicker of light in the peephole before the door opened. This time, however, Myra invited me in.

"Find her?" she asked. There was a comfortable smell in the apartment, the odor of food freshly prepared, and a radio somewhere in the back was softly tuned to a station offering bouncy Latin music. I had an image of her humming to herself as she puttered around the kitchen, happy and calm and domestic, turning the making of a meal into something profoundly satisfying. I realized that Jocelyn had avoided Myra's friendship because people who find happiness in simple, ordinary things also are capable of detecting other elemental states of mind. Over time, Myra would have sniffed out treachery. Indeed, that had already started to happen. *Be aware of girls without girlfriends.*

"Not yet," I said. "I wanted to ask you a couple more things."

The music on the radio stopped and an urgent Spanish voice came on. Myra saw me cock my ear toward it. "Do you speak Spanish?" she asked.

I shook my head. "Neither do I," she said. "It's fun to listen to, though. But have you ever noticed how angry everyone seems to be when they speak it? And they talk so fast. You live in Miami long enough, you realize Americans are just about the slowest-talking people on earth."

It reminded me of a saying I'd once heard. "It's like what the Southern fellow told the guy from New York. It's not that we talk slow, it's just that you listen too fast."

She grinned. "What did you want to ask me?"

"I'm trying to learn something about Geechee. I spent the day at the library but couldn't find anything. What else can you tell me about it?"

"Why do you want to find her that bad?' she asked, ignoring the question.

I considered how to answer. "Because she took something of mine," I said after a moment. It was, as Manzini might say, essentially true.

"Maybe it's best that you don't even look for her. You might be happier not knowing things." She didn't even pretend to believe me.

"No, I need to find her," I said, trying to sound both determined and detached. Perhaps she thought I meant to hurt her; they may not have been pals, but they were sisters, and women learned long ago to be wary of the other beasts. "In fact, I don't really need to even talk to her. I just need to know where she is."

She didn't believe that either. "You find her, you'll be talking to her." But she must have satisfied herself that my intentions, if not honorable, were at least harmless. "Mostly you find those Geechees on the islands around Savannah. Up in South Carolina, some, and down in Georgia. Harder and harder to find them, though. No way to make a living there. And they keep building rich homes everywhere. Somebody comes in, pays some old Geechee family a fortune for their land and they move away. They go to the city, mostly, and start talking like everybody else and pretty soon the little ones start wanting basketball shoes like everybody else and then it's all gone. Then they're just like everybody else."

"These Geechees. Are they black folks?"

She gave me an incredulous look. "Well, yeah. Of course."

"They're sort of like the Gullahs, then?"

"They're not sort of like them. They *are* them. It's just two words for the same bunch of people."

I was confused. "How can Jocelyn be a Geechee, then?"

"Well, honey, I didn't mean it literally. I just meant that she obviously grew up around them. There's lots of white folks on those islands too. She picked up some of that Geechee talk. That's all I meant."

Great. Instead of getting a clue that would have narrowed the search area, exactly the opposite had happened: I now had a several-hundred-mile coastline to explore. I made one last attempt.

"So which of those islands is the most mixed?" I asked. *Mixed?* Jesus. I had all the grace of Bull Conner. Why didn't I just ask her to show me a few dance steps too?

But Myra was unperturbed. "Hard to say. There's a lot more of you than there is of us, you know." Then she gave me a sly smile, to let me know she'd heard. "All those little white babies. Can't you people control yourselves?"

■

The plane turned northward just moments after the beach had appeared as a thin, white line directly below us. The pilot seemed to plant the tip of the port wing on some invisible point of sky, then pivot to the left as he continued to climb, giving me a long look as the city was washed in the promise of a new day. Somewhere below me was Laney Pritchard, nursing a wounded reputation. Perhaps Jocelyn was down there, too. After all, she didn't need to run. There were millions of people living in that mélange of impenetrable communities, whole, vast areas where she could burrow and I could never search. One of us was her enemy, either Laney or I, and maybe she felt it was wise to stay close. You need not always keep loved ones in sight, but adversaries must be watched carefully.

The cause, however, would be elsewhere. And Laney would not search for it, because his complaint was with the *Post-Star.* His lawyer clearly didn't believe our assertions that a mysterious third party had affected everything, much as a black hole in space bends everything toward its invisible mass. He didn't care about our pitiful excuses. He was required to address only what appeared in the paper. How it got there was our problem, and it didn't matter much anyway: You can't suck the bullets back into the barrel. So it was left to us, to me, to find the cause, to look for her.

But I heard her voice in my ear first.

I had fallen asleep shortly after the plane left Miami, lulled by the drone of the engines and the hiss of the fresh-air vents over each seat, all of them opened wide in a faint effort to fight the humidity that had been locked in the cabin with us. I slept uneasily, twitching awake every once in a while when the plane hit a pothole in the sky, but still somehow dreamed. Jocelyn spoke to me of incomprehensible things in my sleep, her voice clear and her breath warm in my ear but her words confusing. I shook myself awake at one point and found a flight attendant next to me, her face squinched in concern.

"Sorry," I muttered, wondering if I'd been talking in my sleep. She smiled and padded her way up the aisle, keeping the tray of filled coffee cups she held on a careful, even keel.

I looked around and took inventory. It was a direct flight to Atlanta, and at least half of my fellow passengers seemed to be men in suits. They were corporate executives, no doubt, and had left their homes before dawn so that they could be in Atlanta by the start of the business day. Many of them had lowered the little tables from the backs of the seats in front of them, and were busy with spreadsheets and reports, making small, precise notes in margins and occasionally attacking their calculators with single-finger punches. I envied the way they were able to deal with treachery and deceit in their businesses: marshaling columns of numbers to make their case and confronting their enemies in quiet memos seen by only a few dozen people. Their missteps would not be paraded past hundreds of thousands of readers.

A few minutes later, the same flight attendant made her way back down the aisle, collecting the remains of her earlier offerings. Her voice, indistinct except for its initial inflection, became clearer as she got closer. By the time she reached my aisle, I realized it had not been a dream at all.

"Are you finished, sir?" she asked the man next to me. He dropped a coffee cup and wadded napkin into the bag she held. I had nothing to give, but still got a wary smile. I suspected I had become the object of a whispered warning to the other attendants as they gathered in the galley. *An odd one in 24C.*

"Thank you," she said to the man, then moved on.

The voice was Jocelyn's. The sound, the cadence, the pronunciation, all of it was hers. But it was somehow more vivid, as if the flight attendant's was the purer version. I tried to listen as she worked her way through the rows, but the murmurs around me had already begun to overcome it.

I waited a few minutes, then turned to look toward the back of the plane. She had finished collecting trash and was standing in the galley with another attendant. I reached up and pushed the call button over my seat.

Neither of them responded for several long minutes, making sure I understood they were professionals and not just sky-bound waitresses who could be waved over. When one of them finally arrived, she was the wrong one.

"Yes, sir?" she said, smiling but not meaning it.

"Could I have a cup of coffee, please?" And have your friend bring it, I thought.

"I'm sorry, sir. The drink cart and coffee pots have all been secured. We're starting our descent to Atlanta." This time her smile was maliciously sincere.

As if on cue, the pilot came on the intercom system and confirmed her claim, using precisely the same words. It made me wish there was a truth-in-flying law that governed in-flight announcements: "Ladies and gentlemen, we're beginning our controlled collision with earth, which is of course the most dangerous part of the journey. Also, my copilot failed his last training session on the flight simulator and, frankly, I think he's hung over this morning. It's seventy-eight degrees in Atlanta under clear skies. It is a good day to die."

I didn't see the attendant for the rest of the flight. I dawdled in the plane after it had pulled up to the terminal, waiting for the cabin to empty before getting up from my seat, stretching ostentatiously and finally opening the overhead bin to retrieve my bag. Still, she didn't appear. I walked slowly to the front of the plane, nodded as yet another attendant recited the airline's official thanks for my patronage, then made my way up the ramp to the terminal. I sat in the closest empty seat and waited.

She appeared ten minutes later, walking with two other attendants and pulling a bag on a small, wheeled cart behind her. She didn't see me until I stood up as she walked by. Alarm showed in her eyes.

"Excuse me," I said, trying to sound harmless, "but I have an odd question. Where are you from? You sound exactly like someone I know."

Her companions hovered protectively as she regarded me, wondering why I asked. Finally she answered. "A little place over on the coast. Reynaud's Landing. It's an island, actually."

"Is there a family named Pritchard there?"

She brightened a bit. "Oh, yeah. There are Pritchards all over. I knew a bunch of them."

"Do you know Jocelyn Pritchard?"

"Oh, sure. I was best friends with one of her cousins." Reassured that nothing was amiss, the other two women drifted off a few steps and began talking. "Jocelyn was older than me, so I didn't know her well. Is she a friend of yours?"

"Yeah, although it's been a while since I've talked to her." Four days, to be precise. "Does she still live there?"

"How funny you ask. I was visiting my mama two days ago and saw Jocelyn in the village."

"Did you talk to her?" I said, wondering how many more questions I could ask and still sound casual.

"Nah. Just saw her across the street and waved. She had the kids with her."

The kids? I wanted to know more, but the answer to my next question drove it from my mind.

"By the way, do you know a fellow named Laney Pritchard?"

"Sure," she said. "He's Jocelyn's brother."

■

Ladies and gentlemen of the jury: I know I come to you late in the process. The evidence is overwhelming and the verdict likely will be quick. I was careless in my judgments, childlike in my credulousness, driven by misplaced righteousness, and all too willing to believe that love can materialize out of sand on a beach. It takes a special person to manage such havoc, and I was that person: angry, arrogant, lonely, messianic, needy. If there was a misstep to be made, I made it. Guilty as charged.

So I don't seek to evade punishment. In fact, the sentence already has been passed. There is a sole thing in life I do well, and that is the preparation of 750 words for publication in a newspaper. But that career ended in just a few seconds as I stood in the middle of an airline concourse and watched a trio of flight attendants walk away. It ended because I wanted it to end. There was a choice to be made at that moment and I made it.

This revelation in the airport was a critical moment, you see. I had discovered a toehold. This was either a scheme or a vendetta between a brother and a sister, with me as the unwitting participant in either event. I could have simply returned to Miami, made my way to Manzini's office, told him what I'd found and been done with it. Quarles would have taken over from there. He would have tested this shred of evidence on Laney Pritchard's claim, gingerly at first, then more and more forcefully until he had carved away as much of the claim as possible.

But would we have learned what was at the root of all this, discovered the truth behind the appearance? Assuredly not. Lawyers treat truth as a volatile and dangerous substance— something used to club an opponent into submission, or something that menaces your own explanations and prevarications. It has no value by itself. If I had turned over my shred of evidence, Quarles would have used it only as a weapon. And I would not have gotten even a shred of enlightenment in return.

So I'll stipulate the argument, as those same lawyers would say. I chose to neglect my duty and responsibility. As I stood in that airport concourse and watched the flight attendants depart, no doubt happily remarking on the surprisingly small na-

ture of the world, I made my decision. I never called Manzini.
In fact, I returned to the *Post-Star* only once, to collect a few
belongings a couple weeks later. But even from a distance I
could feel his fury grow as the ten days passed, could sense his
need to unleash his Dobermans—on me, on Laney Pritchard,
on somebody. He eventually did, after my disappearance had
become undeniable and after Laney's attorney had used that
disappearance as his final lever, hinting darkly to the court that
the *Post-Star*'s inability to make me available for interrogation
was just more evidence of its massive indifference and neglect.
Quarles' estimate was dead-on, as it turned out; the *Post-Star*
eventually agreed to pay Laney Pritchard $3 million and pub-
lish a long article explaining, as best it could, how this decent,
God-fearing, uniquely valuable man came to be so brutally
abused in the newspaper. There was a perverse echo from a
previous story—where is Tad Beckman?—but it was a minor
reference, a terse aside noting that I wasn't present for my own
firing. That annoyed Manzini the most, no doubt: What plea-
sure is there in killing a dead man?

I made my choice. I chose Jocelyn. I gambled on the hope
that amid the deceit there had been one true thing between us.
So what I want now from the court of public opinion, from
those of you who bring distance and compassion to the proceedings, who sit in the warm and comfortable chairs of the
jury box and have the utter luxury of time to mull things as
you wish, is an approving nod. That's all. I'm a happy man
these days, but not so confident in my happiness that I couldn't
benefit from the understanding of others. I made the right
choice, but being right came at a perverse price: It made me see
how bad my previous choices had been.

■

The rental car was in the middle of a vast, orderly row of
Chryslers, all of them identical models and distinguishable only

by their color. The Georgia sun, while still in the young part of the sky, had burned through the windshield with enough determination to make the steering wheel too hot to touch. I started the car, turned its air-conditioning on high, then got out again and leaned against the fender to wait for it to stop pretending to be a pottery kiln.

I had picked up a state highway map at the rental counter. Unfolding it, I studied the coast but couldn't find Reynaud's Landing. I turned the map around, found it in the index, then tracked it down by using the letter-and-number grid along the map's edges.

It was a dot on a small bit of land that had peeled away from the coast between St. Catherines Island and the mainland. It didn't seem to be an island at all, actually, which is why I missed it initially; it was instead a twitch in the coastline separated from the rest of the state by a marsh or creek so shallow and thin that the mapmaker's hand wasn't steady enough to note it. The words "Reynaud's Lndng" were in the smallest type possible, and the map's legend told me that meant it had no more than five hundred people. The legend also said the road leading to it was paved, but was a bare step above a dirt track. Having driven on countless similar roads throughout the state, I could imagine it: a narrow, macadam ribbon with neither shoulders nor a stripe down its middle, all but ignored by the county road department.

It would be a long drive from Atlanta. One interstate highway would take me to Macon, another to Savannah and yet another south along the coast. Then I would have to find the closest exit and weave my way through the salt marshes, hoping that a storm hadn't washed a road out or that an errant shrimp boat captain hadn't disabled a bridge by nudging it in a careless moment as he returned home. With luck, I could be there by late afternoon.

A complete scene worked itself out in my imagination as I

studied the map: Jocelyn would come into the village in the waning hour of the day, perhaps to get a cold drink at the store or to walk to the end of the pier and pass a few calm minutes with the fishermen and crab catchers, who place their faith in the notion that the best hauls are had in half-light. I would be lounging in front of the store, leaning insouciantly against one of the posts holding up the canopy; or maybe I would be sitting on the top of the three steps leading to the door, elbows propped on my knees and eyes narrowed against the sun. She wouldn't recognize me at first. With an old, billed cap pulled low on my head and ragged shorts and shirt, I would look like a boat hand from a nearby village waiting for his buddy inside to finish negotiations for the purchase of beer. But as she got close, she would peer at my face, wondering why this familiar stranger smirked with such confidence.

I would wait for recognition to register before I spoke, and in that instant when her eyes widened, I would say, "I forgot. Were we supposed to meet at my place or yours?" My tone would be ironic and detached.

Jocelyn, of course, would be fearful, ashamed and guilty. She would squat on the step at my feet and stumble through an explanation. I would just stare at her. Then she would realize what she had lost, and would ask if we could return to the way things used to be. I'm not cruel; I wouldn't make her beg. But she would have to demonstrate the depth of her regret, and the demonstration somehow would involve the shedding of clothes. That is, after all, a man's preferred form of apology.

I savored the image for a long moment before folding the map and getting back in the car. It had won its battle with the sun, and the cool air brought me back to reality. I wouldn't blend into a coastal village—newsrooms had left me too pale for that—and I knew any flat stare would come from Jocelyn, not me. She had shown her strength by leaving, even if she'd left a trail for me to follow.

I pointed the car north, toward Barrington and Doralee. I would obey the fundamentals of investigation. I would learn everything I could before the denouement, and the trail led to Almo.

■

I had not visited when my grandfather died. I had finished the funeral arrangements by phone—there was little to do aside from confirming what had already been done, since death is as ritualistic as life in small towns—and driven directly to the service from the Atlanta airport. A neighbor had secured the house, disconnecting appliances and locking doors and windows, and I had arranged for his high school–aged son to make a twice-monthly visit to the yard with his bush hog, a husky brush-cutting blade mounted behind his father's tractor. In return, I gave them the grazing rights to the acre between my grandfather's house and the road, allowing them to string barbed wire along its edges to keep their few cows away from traffic. Nothing demanded that I visit the house, so I hadn't.

I realized, as I drove to Almo's store, how many years had passed since I'd last been there. Homes that I remembered as dilapidated and ramshackle had fresh coats of paint and new shutters, while other homes I had envied—places whose apparent care had suggested to my child's eye a certain order and affection among their inhabitants—now seemed unkempt. Some were much closer to the road than I remembered, their enormous lawns somehow shrunk to mortal size, while the Barton place—which had been built puzzlingly close to the road and served for years as the local bus stop for schoolchildren, including me—had disappeared behind a screen of shrubbery and scrub pine. It had been a place of torment for me one year when some of my classmates had finally tuned into their parents' whisperings and started calling me "Jew boy," refusing to let me in the games they played as they waited for the bus and explaining to the younger kids how I, or at least my ancestors, had killed Jesus. The littlest ones were only then beginning to understand about Jesus, and their horror at my role in his epic death was clear. My protestations and explanations to my classmates had led only to a Hobson's choice—well, then, was I a Jew or a bastard?—and my solicitations of comfort at home had led only to a helpless shrug from my mother and a triumphant, I-told-you-so look for her from my grandfather.

I slowed as I drove past my grandfather's house, but didn't turn in. I would come back later. But even then, I still wouldn't see what Jocelyn had seen in just one night.

■

"Hey, did that gal ever catch up to you?" Almo asked when I walked in the store.

I should have expected no other greeting. Almo was legendary for his refusal to acknowledge surprise, something I remembered from my youth. Now, years later, I was getting a reminder of his unflappability. He made it seem as if I'd just stepped out for a few moments and missed a visitor.

"What woman?" I asked unnecessarily.

"Been by your grandfather's place yet?" he said. This was another of Almo's characteristics: Conversations tended to shift abruptly, with the connections between his questions and comments becoming apparent only later on.

"Nah, I'll go by later. What woman?" I asked again.

"Seen your mother?"

I would have to wait him out. "I've got a few days. I'm going to go see her."

"That was quite a little stir you created." His droopy eyelid dipped in salute.

"Listen, after that writer talked to you, I was an afterthought,"

I said. "It's a shame you didn't know he was coming. You could have dropped a Vienna sausage in the pickle jar and told him it was your finger."

Almo grinned. "Did I ever tell you what happened to my finger?"

"Lots of times."

"Dark-haired woman. Didn't tell me her name, or if she did I don't remember. Said she was a friend from college, or something."

We were back to the main subject. "When was this?"

"A few months back. Four, maybe five." She had settled next to me on the beach that first time almost three months ago; so she'd been here before that. This was my initial clue that I had been studied carefully, that my paths had been patiently charted.

"Dark hair?" I said, prompting him.

He nodded. "Good-looking. Lots of juice in her. Thirties, maybe, although at first I thought she was younger." His tone made me think there was more.

"Why did she stop here?"

"She said she couldn't find your grandfather's house. Said she had directions, but couldn't find it." Among my grandfather's peculiarities was his refusal to put a house number on the mailbox post. "So she stopped in to ask."

"Didn't you tell her the place was empty?" My grandfather had died by then and my mother already had become a permanent resident of the state's happy farm.

"Yeah. But she said she'd leave a note there for you."

I shrugged. "Well, I suppose I'll go by and check."

"There's one other thing," Almo said. "I think she stayed awhile."

"Stayed around here?"

"No. I mean stayed in your grandfather's house."

"You mean she broke in?"

Almo nodded. "I'm pretty sure. When I went past your

grandfather's house on my way home that night, I noticed a car there. It was pulled way around back, like it was meant to be out of sight. I was going to call the neighbor when I got home, but a minute later I came on an accident, a little one, as it turned out. But by the time I'd stopped to make sure nobody was hurt, it got pushed out of my mind. I didn't remember it 'til she came back the next day and I realized it was the same car."

"She came back?"

"Filled up the tank. When she came in to pay, I asked her if she'd found you. She said, 'Sort of,' and just gave me an odd little smile. I stopped by the house that night, but it was all locked up. And everything seemed fine when I looked through the windows."

She had simply done what was required of any serious hunter: She'd visited the places where the creature had rested, looking for clues to its habits and routines. If you do this with sufficient deliberation and care, you learn what the creature best responds to.

I pointed to the small, oblong tray nestled against the cash register. "I'll bet she took a pack of matches, didn't she?"

For the first time ever, I saw surprise register on Almo's face. "How did you know?"

CHAPTER FOURTEEN

Nature had moved to reclaim its territory. The bushes and vines around the foundation of the house had sent countless search parties up its walls, while the leaves and twigs that clotted the gutters had given birth to the rot that would eventually claim the roof. The paint had announced its intention to peel by bubbling up in several dozen places, and one shutter had almost succeeded in an escape attempt, but remained crookedly captured by a single, dogged nail. The floorboards of the front porch had a spongy feel under my feet.

The lock in the door put up a fight before I remembered that you had to pull the doorknob toward you as the key was turned. I stepped inside and shut the door behind me. It had been years since I'd been in the house, and I could immediately smell my mother's absence: The odor was that of a place where food had been badly prepared and the cleaning had been haphazard and infrequent, the mark of a man who lives alone. I could see her absence too. As I walked by her bedroom, I saw that it had been stripped of everything except a bed frame and chest of drawers. My grandfather, it seemed, had not expected her to return.

Otherwise, things looked much the same as I remembered them. My grandfather may not have been scrupulously clean, but he was tidy. Two pairs of shoes were set neatly next to his bed, each shoe perfectly adjacent to its mate and all of them nestling their toes against the same invisible line. Newspapers were in an orderly stack beside his chair, and a half-dozen *Reader's Digest*s were fanned out on a nearby table, arranged in careful chronological order with the oldest on the left. The furniture was arranged with a Shaker's sense of symmetry, with chests set precisely in the center of walls, chairs pushed squarely under a dining room table that itself sat at dead center of the room, blinds all cocked at exactly the same angle, and accent pillows allotted with tedious attention to ratio: one each for the living room chairs, two for the love seat and three for the couch, all of them set fussily against the back cushions. Drinking glasses stood at permanent attention in the kitchen cupboard, while carving knives in the drawer were all laid with their sharp edges facing the same way.

I was never to touch his things. Every room had held its own prohibitions: chairs not to sit on, coffee cups not to drink from, drawers never to explore, towels never to use on my unwelcome little body. The house had been my universe, and although it had seemed like a vast space, there was only a grudging corner of it available to me. My mother had moved more easily through his world because she was of him; but somehow the genetic bond had not seemed to pass along to the next generation. Now, despite an accumulation of years and his death, the house's order remained intimidating.

Not so for Jocelyn. She had set out to learn what she could about me, and found something else unexpectedly interesting in a desk or cabinet. She then had begun mining my grandfather's papers and files for similar tidbits, and eventually pieced the whole puzzle together. Having no history in the house—feeling no uneasiness about violating its tidiness—and probably not trusting me to discover what I had not seen for so many years, she had left it all on the kitchen table for me. But even then, I didn't see what she had seen. It was just a familiar, unhappy recounting of my mother's problems, the official record of her madness. I was blind to what had been so clear to Jocelyn. Blind, that is, until Jack the dog visited my dreams two days later, calling to me as piteously as Lady had called from the tree.

She left something else for me, something she had not found in the house but instead brought with her to place on top of the pile of papers. It was a highway map, the twin of the one I had that day acquired at the airport. It was folded oddly, counter to its creases so that the coastline faced up, and a red ink circle had been drawn on the map, looped around several times in the way one does to draw the eye emphatically to a certain spot. In the circle was Reynaud's Landing.

If you have found this, Tad, if you are so clever and needy as to have gotten this far, you'll need to go a bit farther.

■

Cooley exaggerated his surprise as much as Almo hid his. He made a great show of letting his jaw drop and announcing to the newsroom as I walked in: "Attention everyone! We have a star journalist among us."

Everyone stared. I recognized perhaps half the faces in the room, while the others—including an earnest young woman sitting at my old desk who talked on the phone even as she tried to follow the commotion around her—were new. I made my own show of studying the newsroom as a general inspects his troops, turning my gaze slowly from one side to the other and pursing my lips in concentration.

"That's Mr. Star Journalist to you," I finally said to Cooley.

"Did you forget something?" he asked, ignoring me. "Your dignity? Your self-respect? Your Pulitzer prize?"

"I forgot what a grouchy old bastard you are."

"I'm not old," Cooley said in mock protest. Everything else apparently was beyond argument.

"I need your help with something," I said.

"You can ignore my advice over the phone. You didn't have to come here to ignore it in person."

"I didn't say advice. I said help."

He shrugged. "I'll see what I can do. Let's go sit down."

He led me to his office. I pulled the photograph of Jocelyn from an oversized envelope and set it on his desk. Cooley spoke first.

"Do you know her?"

"Yeah," I said. "Why?"

"She was here a few months ago. I talked to her for quite a while."

I heard an echo of my conversation with Almo the previous day. "Did she mention me?"

"Don't be so full of yourself," Cooley said. "Your name didn't come up. Usually doesn't, unless some goddamn Yankee writer's in town."

"What did she want?"

"Why do you ask?" Newspapering will do that to you: You never give anything away without having learned something first.

I told him. My recounting to Manzini had been careful and incomplete, with only the detail necessary to make him understand that a conspiracy was afoot and that Jocelyn was at its center, but not so much as to make him see my emotional investment. But Cooley was uninvolved, so his detachment could be valuable. Besides, I owed him something. Confessing to current sins seemed like a way to atone for previous ones.

He was a gentle and forgiving listener. He cropped the incredulity from his voice when posing questions and murmured sympathetically at those moments when it was clear that the flesh was still tender. He refused to let us be interrupted, dismissing one visitor behind me with a shake of his head and answering the phone with a guttural, "Not now." The next day's edition of the *Chronicle* was making its ponderous way toward the pressroom, but if he was concerned that it would lurch in his absence, he gave no sign. Mine was the story of the day.

Compassionate as he was, however, Cooley would not pat me on the head and reassure me.

"You've got a problem," he said at the end.

"You know, you've got a real gift for insight," I said. "It's amazing how you can get right to the heart of the matter."

He refused to be baited. "You've got a problem because you don't know what I know."

"What do you know?"

"Look, you clearly want this woman"—he gestured at the photograph, which still lay on his desk—"to be a victim in all this, as much as you are. But that's not the case."

"How can you be so sure?" Despite the previous day's evidence of her campaign, I was still willing to be wrong.

"I don't think she was in here that day to see me. I was an impulse. She'd spent several hours in the archive. I don't know what she was doing, exactly. But as she was leaving, she stuck her head in my door, bold as you please, and introduced herself. Said she was working on a graduate thesis and wondered if she could ask me a few things. She was here quite a while. Clever girl. I liked her."

"What did she ask you about?"

Cooley stared for a moment before answering. "Libel law," he finally said.

"Oh, great," I said, slumping down in my chair.

"She'd already done a lot of work," he continued. "Knew all the major cases. *Times* versus *Sullivan*. *AP* versus *Walker*. But they all deal with public figures, of course, and that wasn't what she was interested in. She said she was studying how ordinary people fared when they took libel complaints to the courts."

"So you loaded the gun for her."

"I didn't know," he said, and I noticed his voice had taken

on its own tone of confession. "She asked a lot of specific questions. Does the simple publication of a mistake constitute libel? Do you have to show that a newspaper set out to smear you? What makes a public figure? What's the worst possible set of circumstances for a newspaper?"

I could imagine Jocelyn sitting in the same seat I now occupied, leading Cooley through the questions until she learned exactly what she needed to do. "What did you tell her?"

"About the worst situation?" he asked. I nodded. "I told her this would be as bad as it gets: A newspaper publishes something that is clearly and provably untrue. The story has an immediate and direct negative financial effect on the person being written about. It is shown that the information was gathered recklessly and carelessly. And it is shown that the newspaper had been warned in advance that the article was wrong." He hesitated, as if there was something else that he preferred not to add.

"Yeah, and . . . ?"

"And that the writer is shown to have had a personal vendetta."

There it was. Cooley had unknowingly given her a blueprint, had described in detail exactly what needed to happen to make Laney's lawsuit bulletproof. And Jocelyn had scrupulously observed the formula. In fact, her snare was as cleverly constructed as a Chinese finger trap: My columns, and the mistakes they harbored, could be forgiven or at least explained by the notion that I had sought to protect the helpless; but protection had become consortium and conspiracy, and citing one as a defense inevitably led to a charge of the other. She had known precisely what she needed me to do, and had systematically led me to it. It was perversely fitting that the instructions had come from Cooley, whose advice I had ignored so many times before.

We sat without speaking for a few moments. Finally, I leaned over Cooley's desk and tapped the object under Jocelyn's arm in the photograph. "I need to find out about this."

Cooley's surprise wasn't exaggerated this time. "You really don't remember?" he asked.

■

The newspaper had been folded so that its identity was only partially evident, with the last two letters of the city's name and first three of the paper's name visible. Tucked under her arm, it was unimportant to the photograph, just one of several minor details that gave it an ineluctable sense of place and moment: the clock over her shoulder attached to the terminal wall, the cultist with the carnations in the background, the video monitors that make their fraudulent declarations of on-time flight performance. The photograph wanted you to look at her, at her tears and sadness. Everything else was just there.

But I had noticed the newspaper name. In the *Post-Star*'s lobby that morning, in the moment before Emile waved me over to his desk to tell me Mr. Manzini would be right down, it was the newspaper that had registered in my mind. At the time, I was pretty sure it was the Barrington *Chronicle* being carried by this sad woman; the visible portions of the name matched, as did the typeface. It was only mildly curious, though, the sort of coincidence—like encountering an acquaintance on the street of a faraway city—that life occasionally offers to keep you alert. I didn't know the sad woman then, of course, and the mental note I made to examine the picture more closely later was almost immediately buried when Manzini, himself another coincidence, appeared in the lobby. When the mental note inexplicably resurfaced the day Laney and his lawyer visited, when it suddenly demanded that I hunt down the photograph and examine it anew, there lurked yet another coincidence: I knew the sad woman now. But her possession of a copy of the Barrington *Chronicle* could not be an accident.

But here the mind does a strange thing. The headline on that day's front page—itself, like the name of the paper, only partly evident—didn't register. My memory refused to acknowledge what Cooley saw almost right away, an oversight so profound that it could only have been subconsciously deliberate. The headline was all I needed to know, but something deep within me didn't wish to know it.

I wonder if she knew. Did she awaken every morning knowing that somewhere in the *Post-Star* building was a photograph that could lead to the unmasking of her charade? How often did she wonder whether I would come across it? Did she end every day with thanks for having come one step closer to the end without complication?

Maybe she didn't know at all. She had brushed by the photographer, refusing to give her name, so the mystery of her identity and circumstances had become a handicap for the photo editor. Unable to explain to readers why she wept, he'd relegated her to the bottom of the page, a small tile in the photo mosaic that carried the title "A Day in the Life of the Airport" across two facing pages in the middle of the Sunday paper. That was the day, perhaps, that still in the grip of her grief she had merely set the newspaper aside. And what's not seen doesn't exist.

Cooley led me to the *Chronicle*'s archive. We stood before a massive bank of drawers containing decades' worth of newspapers, each article from each edition carefully trimmed, sorted by name and subject, and crammed into manila envelopes.

"Do you remember the name?" he asked.

"No," I said, after thinking a moment.

Cooley shook his head. "Then we'll never find it here. When did you leave?"

After I told him, we went instead to the wall that held the full-sized, bound copies of the paper. Working back from my departure date, we soon found a copy of the paper Jocelyn carried. Then, working forward, we found the subsequent reports and, with them, Jocelyn's and Laney's names. They were indeed listed as brother and sister.

Cooley not only had given me the how, he'd supplied the why.

■

There was one more visit to make before I went to Reynaud's Landing.

The same attendant met me in the hallway and escorted me to her door, but this time he told me just to look through the window and not go in.

"She sleeps during the day now," he said, "and stays awake all night. It's sort of like she works third shift."

"Why do you let her do that?" They were supposed to be treating her, not accommodating her madness.

"What does it matter when people sleep? It helps her a lot." The words were gentle, but his tone was unmistakable: If I'd delegated kindness to him, what was my job?

"When does she wake up?" I asked.

"Right before dark."

"I'll come back."

"Once you get inside the gate, just come straight here," he said. "The door will be locked, but if you ring the bell outside, Buford will come get you. It'll take him a few minutes, though, so be patient."

I indeed skipped the required check-in at the administrative building that night and went directly to my mother's dormitory. I pushed the buzzer by the entrance and waited a long time until a huge shape appeared behind the opaque, wire-reinforced glass set into the door.

"You Miz Collie's boy?" the attendant asked after opening the door. I nodded.

"My man told me you might come. Let's go upstairs."

I followed him into the building and through several sets of locked doors. He was enormously large, with the bulk of a football player who has stopped training but kept eating, yet he stepped lightly down the hallways, agile and confident. He hesitated at numerous rooms to peer inside or just listen, combining his escort of me with his making of the rounds. The ward was still and dim, with many of the overhead lights having been turned off and only the occasional cough or cry coming from within the rooms. Insanity slept well that night, it seems. A few times he scratched notes on a small notebook he fished from his shirt pocket.

Finally we reached the desk in the alcove on my mother's floor. The door to the cage that separated it from the hall was open, and she sat in a chair adjacent to the desk, holding a few playing cards in her hand. The rest of the deck was on the desk, sitting in a circle of light beamed down from a gooseneck lamp.

"Look what I found scratching at the door," the attendant said.

"Hey, baby," my mother said. She stood and we hugged.

"You all go on down to your room to talk," the attendant said to my mother. "We'll just deal this hand over again. I ain't got squat anyway." To me he added: "You came at a good time. She's already up two million dollars."

"Two and a half million," she corrected.

"Ain't you the sharp one. But I'm going to stop letting you cheat." His grin was genuine.

She had settled into her room since I'd last visited. She'd somehow acquired a couple of lamps, which, along with the overhead light, were already switched on when we went in, giving the room a midday brightness. A square of lace was draped over the dresser, and there were dozens of pages from home magazines taped to the walls, all of them carefully cut and all of them picturing variations of the same thing: showcase rooms stuffed with pricey furniture, with sunlight pouring in from oversized windows. Next to the bed was an extra pair of shoes, primly placed there as if my grandfather himself had done it. The sight of them gave me an uncomfortable moment as I wondered if some bits of his genetic code had been passed through her to me after all.

She settled into an armchair in the corner while I perched on the edge of the bed. "I want to talk to you about something," I said, deciding just to plunge in. "I want you to tell me about the monster that took your baby."

My mother smiled unexpectedly. "That's exactly what your friend wanted me to talk about, too."

CHAPTER
FIFTEEN

Reynaud's Landing was something else I was wrong about. The road leading to it was a new, smooth four-lane highway, built on a long causeway through the coastal salt marsh. It was mid-morning as I made my way east, and the fishermen who gathered at the bridges where the road crossed channels of water were already packing their tackle and tossing leftover bits of bait over the railing, an act that was both a reward to the fish for its elusiveness and a nurturing of its feeding habit: Tomorrow's lunge at that fat minnow may not be so free of consequence. About halfway across the causeway, a parking area bulged out into the marsh, a spot where drivers could pull over and read the historic marker placed there. I stopped and learned that 250 years previous, a company of Highlanders had chosen that bog to meet a Spanish incursion from Florida, dressing in their red woolen uniforms and lining up in the summer heat to hold firm against an army that wished to claim the nearby earthen fort protecting the river inlet. The marker's carefully neutral language, which suggested that the Spaniards were just another set of exploiters whose greatest sin was to arrive late and not have enough men, clashed with my schoolboy's memory of the same history, which had brave Anglo-Saxon soldiers keeping the colonies safe from swarthy papists. Of course, had they known what would develop, the Scots could have just pointed the way to Miami or east Los Angeles and pocketed the cost of ammunition.

Just before the road reached the island, it humped up over the Intracoastal Waterway, giving me a look at a marina that had begun making room for yachts and deep-sea fishing boats among the shrimpers and trawlers. When the road touched ground again, a sign welcomed me to Reynaud's Landing and a cluster of directional arrows beneath it pointed me toward the beaches, village, resort and marina. The arrows for the village and resort pointed down the same road. I took that one.

Far from being a remote and isolated spit of sand, it was a thriving seaside town that had managed the neat trick of accommodating its growth without worshiping it. Some government body, evidently anticipating the island's eventual discovery, must have crafted a muscular set of zoning restrictions early enough so that when developers finally arrived they simply accommodated the rules rather than fight them. As a result, there wasn't a structure on the island higher than two stories. New homes looked like tidier versions of the original ramshackle cottages, store signs were tucked into little hills next to the street, and the single resort was a sprawling, random collection of buildings that required a five-minute search before I finally located the office.

"Do you have a reservation?" the clerk asked when I inquired about a room.

"Nope," I said.

"How long will you be staying?" he continued.

"A night or two."

"Are you on holiday?" His disapproval was clearly growing by the moment.

"Do I have to pass a test to get a room?" I asked. "It's a pretty simple yes-or-no question: Is there one available?"

He gave me a precious frown. "We're a resort, sir. We're not really set up to handle a short stay. Perhaps you could try the Tradewinds, over in the village."

I found the motel just a mile down the road, one block away from the village's main street. It was a flat-roofed, cinder block building set in the midst of a lawn of crumbling asphalt. The doors of its dozen or so rooms were painted a raucous turquoise, the sort of color that would have given the resort desk clerk the vapors. A neon sign near the street announced that there were vacancies, and the empty parking lot confirmed it.

The motel manager, a fiftyish woman who looked like Ava Gardner would have if she'd stayed in North Carolina and eaten fried food all her life, stood up and eyed me as I walked in. She'd been watching a little black-and-white television that had a square of tinfoil wrapped around its antenna.

"You must be checking in, 'cause we got nobody to check out," she said.

"I guess that means the presidential suite is available," I answered.

"Actually, it ain't. It's on permanent reservation in case he decides to stop in. I can give you the pool suite, though. Or the bridal suite, if you think you might get lucky."

She reminded me of Mrs. Reynolds. I suspected that not much happened beyond this motel office that she didn't know and have an opinion about. And I realized that the sooner I confided in her, the less risk I ran that she'd set out on her own to figure out who I was and why I was there.

"Just let me have your finest room. Could be just a night or two, or"—I tried to sound meaningful—"maybe more."

"Business, huh?" she said. I nodded.

"What sort of work is it you do, exactly?"

"I'm just like anyone else. I buy things and sell things." I said it with as much smug modesty as I could muster.

She gave me a knowing look. "Ain't much around here to buy and sell except land."

I just smiled and filled out the registration card she'd pushed across the desk toward me, leaving a blank space on the line that asked for the name of my company. She scanned it carefully, then shrugged as she filed it away.

"Room four," she said, sliding a key toward me. "And let me ask you something. Why didn't you stay at the resort? Most other businessmen do."

"Yeah, and then you're just hanging around other businessmen. I want to learn something about this town. So that's why I'm here instead."

"You've come to the right place," she said happily. "You just tell me what you need to know."

■

I found the phone book in the nightstand drawer. There were eighteen listings under the name Pritchard, most of them in Reynaud's Landing. A few, however, were located in the nearby communities that weren't large enough to warrant their own phone book, but collectively helped make the listings for Reynaud's Landing seem bulky. There was no Jocelyn Pritchard among the names.

I copied every address. The Pritchards who lived in Reynaud's Landing all seemed to be clumped together on three roads on the island's southern end. It was only noon, and I considered driving there for a look. But I hadn't slept the night before. I had coaxed the story out of my mother and meshed it with the things I'd read, the things Jocelyn had left on the table for me to find. Then, with her tale still fresh in my ears, I had driven straight to Reynaud's Landing. I had gotten close to my mother's truth, had gotten almost near enough to touch it, but in my fatigue it stayed just beyond my reach. There would be no exploration until I slept a bit.

I settled myself on the motel room bed, with the telephone book still open beside me. I dreamed and then I understood.

■

When I awoke, the sun was parked just above the horizon, perhaps an hour away from dipping below it altogether. Earlier, I'd
been too tired to drive to the island's far end; now it was too
late, and I was hungry besides. I jammed my room key in my
pocket and headed for the motel office.

"Find anything to buy yet?" the manager asked when I
walked in. The television was still on.

"I'm thinking about investing in dinner," I said. "Any sug-
gestions?"

She gestured toward the village center. "Two places just a
block away. The Captain's Table is pretty good, if you don't
mind paying too much and having to be friends with the
waiter. Then there's Eddie's. You're fine there if you don't order
anything fried."

"What should I get, then?"

She pretended to ponder for a moment. "Bowl of cereal's
your best bet. He's too lazy to learn to cook properly, so he just
drops everything into the deep-fry. Never changes the oil, either. And he's ugly too."

I had to laugh. "What do you figure Eddie says when someone asks him if there's a nice motel nearby?"

"I know exactly what he says. He's been steering people to
the resort ever since I divorced him."

"I'll tell him you said hello."

"You might want to give the silverware a good look," she
said as I went out. "He ain't too careful about washing."

The village was a two-block-long cluster of stores that ran
perpendicular to the water, with a traffic light at one end and a
small pier at the other. Most of the businesses had the look of
long-established family enterprises, with faded signs and dusty
window displays that were reassuring in a perverse way, suggesting their proprietors had long ago abandoned the trickeries
of marketing to keep customers happy. There was a hardware

store, a pharmacy, a clothing store whose exclusive clientele apparently were elderly women who needed something new for church, a news-and-candy stand, and a gas station that hadn't yet segregated its pumps into a full-serve and self-serve apartheid. There were newer shops too, those that had followed the trickle of tourists to supply them with the things people need to confirm that they're on vacation: a kite shop, an ice cream parlor, a narrow storefront peddling T-shirts and bags of seashells.

I could see both restaurants, the Captain's Table on the water next to the pier and Eddie's in the middle of the second block. I stood for a moment, debating whether I was more interested in a decent meal or amusement, before I noticed the park. I walked over and surveyed it.

It was exactly as Jocelyn had described it the night when we'd rescued the magician. It was adjacent to the water, with a wide lawn and a cluster of playground equipment set into a sandy dip in its middle. At one end was an open-air pavilion, where mothers sat and watched their children with an indulgent eye, while some men were pitching horseshoes nearby and yet others were huddled around the back of a pickup truck, surreptitiously sipping beer. There were dozens of children at play, gathered in companionable groups that broke apart moments after forming in the mystifying social rituals of youth. A few of the adults were clearly visitors, identifiable by their resort clothes and by the nervous way they watched their youngsters, ready to swoop down at the first sign of aggression from the rougher-playing natives. But most were local people, calling across the park to one another, greeting newcomers with a wave and occasionally rearranging their lawn chairs under the pavilion when the gossip dictated a shift. This was the island's social hub. I needn't look for her. She would come to me here.

I waited until well after dark, my hunger forgotten, but she never appeared. I came back the next night, and the four nights after that. I found her on the evening before Manzini's tenth day.

■

I used my time wisely.

I had coffee every morning in the motel lobby, pouring a cup from the pot the manager kept next to a tray of day-old dough-nuts that constituted the free continental breakfast advertised on the sign outside. The first couple of mornings, I leaned against the counter and chatted with the manager, whose name—and I didn't discern whether it was her first or last—was Miggles. By the third morning, I was behind the counter with her, leaning back in a spare chair next to the television and getting a revisionist history of Reynaud's Landing, a voluble stream-of-consciousness recounting that I could occasionally steer but never really corral.

"The whole place was a cotton plantation originally, grow-ing that sea island cotton. You ever seen it? Makes a wonderful fabric. Almost like silk, but irons up real nice. After the war, the land was taken away from the white folks and given to the col-ored folks. The official story was that the plantation had been abandoned, so the federals took it over and gave it to the peo-ple who had stayed around, which of course were the slaves 'cause they had nowhere to go. But the truth is, the Reynaud family was living right there. They didn't have anywhere to go, either.

"It's an interesting story. By the time Sherman got to Savan-nah, there were a lot of loose bands of men roaming around. Some of them federal deserters, some of them local white trash; they'd ride together for a while and plunder. They stayed clear of the regular army, which of course itself was plundering pretty good. But the regular army wasn't murdering anybody except dogs—did you know that?"

I was confused. "Know what? That they killed dogs or didn't murder?"

"The dogs, fool," Miggles said impatiently. "The federals had orders to kill every dog they found, especially tracking dogs. Those poor beasts. There ain't too many innocent people, but animals ain't guilty of anything. One human trains 'em to do something, then another one comes along and kills 'em for it. You can only hope that when Sherman got to heaven, he found out dogs run the place.

"Anyway. One of those groups of bad men found their way here. First they burned down the main house on the plantation. Then they had their way with Reynaud's daughter, and then shot her brother when he tried to stop it. They were having a grand time of it, drinking and carrying on, until one of them realized the slaves were watching everything. It must have been a Southern boy who noticed, some thieving no-account who'd hooked up with this group, and this offended his peculiar sense of propriety. It's one thing to burn down someone's house, rape a young girl and kill a man. That's just an afternoon's sport. But to have a bunch of coloreds maybe enjoying the whole spectacle? Uhuh. That's not to be tolerated.

"So what they did was, they dragged one of those slaves over to a tree, looped a rope around a branch and hung him. Then they just rode off.

"This is where the interesting thing happened. As soon as those riders got out of sight, the white men cut down that slave, kept him from dying up there. And the colored women tended to the Reynaud girl, who'd been beat up pretty bad, too. In other words, they all looked after each other. For one brief moment, they were all just people who had endured a terrible thing together.

"Now, old man Reynaud had been a typical plantation owner, by all accounts. He wasn't particularly brutal, but they weren't all one big happy family, either, like a lot of Southern people try to tell it. He was running a business, and those slaves were just machinery. But he changed his mind pretty quick when he saw what other white people can do, given the chance.

"The Reynauds moved into one of the slave cabins. They took the biggest one, naturally, but still, all the things that had made them the lords of the realm were gone. Anything of any value had been carried off, horses stolen, house burned down, some of the slaves slipped off. So there they were, living like colored folks, wondering what they were going to do.

"Now, one of the slaves was a remarkable old guy named Uncle Giz. He was a clever fellow, apparently. Smart, low-key, make you laugh at the right time, and before you know it he's got you doing something you didn't expect to do. Uncle Giz became the leader of the slaves. They'd figured out things had changed pretty dramatically and maybe they didn't have to do what old man Reynaud said anymore. It was a *Lord of the Flies* thing. This island was real isolated back then—it was a long time before anyone came around—so the social order sort of got reordered.

"But everyone remembered that day when the marauders came, that day when skin color hadn't really counted for much. It became the thing that kept them from killing each other. Old man Reynaud and Uncle Giz became a two-man council. Somehow, they made it work. Reynaud was smart enough to know things were never going to be like they were before. And Uncle Giz was smart enough to know that appearances still counted for something. That the slaves were going to come out of this a lot better off unless they queered it by rubbing the white people's noses in their misfortune.

"So everybody just went back to work. No one knew if there would be a market for cotton, but there were a lot of people to feed, so a huge garden was planted. And they rounded up the farm animals that had been stampeded by the riders. And they salvaged what they could from the big house, digging through the ashes for anything that might be useful. Reynaud was still in charge, more or less, but they were all pretty much doing the same work. Nobody was getting served drinks on the porch anymore.

"After a while, a few months or so, the federals finally got around to visiting. Real troops this time. The war was over by

then, and the soldiers were checking in at the remote planta-
tions. First they asked for Reynaud, but all the white people
were keeping out of sight 'cause they didn't know what the federals had in mind for them. Then the officer looks around, sees
how things have been tended, so he tells Uncle Giz that he and
the other colored people can consider this their land now. That
it had been officially confiscated by the government, and because it was clear they were responsible and industrious, he
could on behalf of the military administrator in Savannah go
ahead and turn over the land to them.

"But still they stuck together. When a land-title official came
by later, to make it all nice and proper, old man Reynaud's
name was quietly listed along with everyone else's.

"Uncle Giz was still being smart about it, you see. Who
knew how long the federal troops would be around to protect
them? White folks eventually were going to come out on top
anyway, so Uncle Giz figured if you had less to take away, the
whites would have less reason to take it away from you.

"He was right, as it turned out. After Reconstruction ended,
most colored folks found themselves with nothing. But old man
Reynaud and Uncle Giz had been working together for so long
that they'd begun to like each other. So everybody just kept the
pieces of land they had and they all farmed together 'til the boll
weevil wiped out the cotton. Then they just switched to other
crops. It was the eighteen-nineties before either one of them
died, and by then there was no arguing about land. All the de-
scendants are still living down there, matter of fact."

"Down where?" I asked.

"On the southern half of the island," Miggles said.

"Are they named Reynaud?"

"Nope. The old man had two sons. One of them got killed
protecting his sister, and the other caught a fever and died just
a year or so later. That just left the girl. Now, here's the last part
of the story: One of those riders came back right after the war
ended. Just rode up one day and confessed to old man Reynaud

that he'd been part of the bunch that raped and killed and stole. Reynaud was going to shoot him on the spot, but Uncle Giz suggested that maybe he should hold off on that, since it seemed to be what this fellow wanted, and what satisfaction was there in giving him what he wants? So Uncle Giz took the rider off and talked to him awhile. It turned out this fellow wasn't much older than a kid, and that he hadn't done the raping and the killing. He'd fallen in with that bunch thinking it would be an adventure, but was horrified by what he'd seen. He couldn't forget it, and he couldn't forgive himself for not trying to stop it. So he'd come back to take his punishment.

"So you know what they did? They told him he would be forgiven if he brought back the man who'd been the leader of the marauders. Damned if this kid didn't track that fellow to the Oklahoma territory and somehow get him back here. They hung that man from a tree next to where the plantation house had stood.

"The kid stayed. He eventually married the Reynaud girl, the one who'd been violated. They both had a lot of grit in them. He'd proved it, of course, by showing up here, then bringing back the killer. But she had it, too. After what happened to her, any other woman of the time would have taken to her room and never come out again. Not her. She said she wasn't going to let those men kill two people. They raised a bunch of kids, all of them just as tough-minded as they were."

"What were their names?" I asked, already knowing the answer.

"Pritchard," she said.

"And they're the ones that still live here?"

She nodded. "Some of them have moved away, naturally, but there's a bunch scattered all over the bottom half of the island. That grit has stayed true through the generations. You cross one of them, you've got all of them to deal with."

■

The library confirmed Miggles's story. Like my morning sessions in the motel office, the library had become a regular part of my routine as I waited for enough time to pass each day before stationing myself at the park's edge. Patience was one of my few remaining virtues.

It was a creaky old place with a bare, plank floor and cast-off furniture, a remote outpost of the county library system whose random assortment of books and periodicals was guarded by a pair of old-lady volunteers. My request for any volumes of local history had sent them flapping off in different directions, each calling questions or encouragement to the other over the stacks until they finally met at one particular shelf and triumphantly waved me over. I joined them and waited as they pulled different books from the shelves and presented them to me, competing for my approval. One of them flourished a picture history of Reynaud's Landing that had been published by a coastal historical society some years before, while the other offered a denser, textbooklike tome that looked like it had afflicted several generations of students before being exiled to the library. Although the picture history was what I wanted, I took them both. Occasionally you give a prize to everyone who enters the race.

As often happens, the most help came from the unlikeliest source. The textbook turned out to be the fruit of a New Deal–era writers' project, a superbly written history of the coastal South. The author apparently had been captivated by the events at Reynaud's Landing, and had made its section one of the longer passages in the book. The children of the characters in the drama Miggles had described would have been elderly by the 1930s, but the author had found them and spent many long hours mining their memories for details on the odd alliance between old man Reynaud and Uncle Giz. The result was a clear-eyed account of how a white planter and a group of former slaves had come to realize that their land was a bond more powerful than the things that divided them. The story of

Hollis Pritchard and the Reynaud daughter was there too, and for both tales the author offered elaboration that made each ring true: for instance, that Pritchard, even after delivering the killer back from Oklahoma, still spent years working at no wage as proof of his atonement, and when acceptance came, it was gradual and grudging; and that old man Reynaud, whose friendship with Uncle Giz was so strong that he once laid a gun to the head of a county tax assessor who had mistakenly and almost fatally believed Reynaud would stand aside while an old ex-slave's property was taken through trickery, was himself not above reacquiring some of the family land from other black families that had fallen on hard times.

In contrast, the picture history was largely useless. There was little text aside from the captions accompanying the photographs, giving the book a jerky feel and making clear the authors didn't view history as a series of related events, but instead as a collection of a few singular moments sprinkled among great years of inactivity. Even the captions themselves managed to evade clarity, written not to impart information so much as to make the families who had contributed photographs feel happy about their antecedents. I counted thirty exclamation points as I leafed through.

I stopped on two facing pages, however. On the left side was a photograph of old man Reynaud and Uncle Giz, seated together on the porch of a house—the book, predictably, failed to tell me whose house, or where it was—dressed in Sunday finery and looking at the camera with stern expressions. The year 1892 was written in a corner of the picture, and the caption explained that the pair were a former master and slave who had become an emblem of racial harmony in the New South!

On the other page was a second photograph, showing three people standing at the edge of a field of cotton. I studied it for a long time. Old man Reynaud was pictured there as well, looking fifteen years younger but with the same unforgiving visage. Next to him was his daughter, who could have been Jocelyn's twin. Her dark hair was barely pinned into submission and her eyes had the same appraising look that Jocelyn's had that morning I first encountered her on the street. The two of them stood together, sleeves touching.

Hollis Pritchard stood to the side, apart from the other two as if the photographer had insisted he step into the picture and he'd done so only reluctantly. And rather than stand next to his wife, he'd placed himself on the other side of old man Reynaud, seeming to want his acknowledgment but uncertain of getting it. His was the look of a man who had done both terrible things and courageous things, and wondered why the second didn't quite make up for the first.

CHAPTER
SIXTEEN

She was sitting, not under the pavilion with the others but across the park under the branches of an enormous live oak tree. The grass was sparse there, and she had spread a blanket to sit on, which even from a distance I could see was the same blanket we had shared many times on other beaches. There was a book beside her, but she ignored it for the many long minutes that I watched her; perhaps the light had grown too dim to read, but it was more likely that the book was the device by which she justified sitting apart from her neighbors. The Pritchards kept to themselves, I had learned.

Eddie proved to be as loquacious as his ex-wife, and his threat to my health overstated. He had scrambled my eggs and scooped grits onto a plate that first morning, sulking only for a few moments when I refused the bacon but otherwise chatting happily the whole time. The clerk at the newsstand next door, which became my third stop every day after Miggles's lobby and Eddie's counter, was almost their equal as he sold me my newspaper. The library ladies were helpful, too, although I took care never to ask for books on a specific subject again. I wasn't certain I could share my favor quite so deftly a second time.

Jocelyn shifted on the blanket, watching the dozen or so children at play. I tried to pick them out, but couldn't. I stood underneath the awning of a store, pondering my approach and feeling silly for doing it. That I was mulling a great opening line was itself part of the problem: I'd spent too much of my life wondering how to fit myself into the world.

A shrimp boat passed the end of the pier, a hundred yards offshore and heading north for the docks on the mainland, where the long digestive process begins. The captain gave a short blast from his horn, followed by a longer one, prompting a wave from several of the seated adults and a great hurrah from the children. She neither waved nor turned to look.

Suddenly the scene took on a staged feel. What I had taken as proof of the peculiar Pritchard nature now seemed like conspicuous visibility. She was a lure. My days of rattling around Reynaud's Landing asking questions had felt like stealthy inquiry at the time, but I apparently had not gone unnoticed. How long had she waited for me to declare my intentions? Had she expected me, like Hollis Pritchard a hundred years earlier, to arrive at the front door and announce that I was there to confront the past? I must have confused her. I hadn't acted impulsively, hadn't thrashed about as a deceived and spurned lover should. Instead, it must have seemed to her that I'd adopted her strategy, that I'd taken on the deliberate calm of a hunter as I patiently studied her history and habits. She didn't know, of course, that I understood now. If I seemed calm, it was because I knew I had never been the real target. I had simply been the device by which she could punish something larger, the tool she used to levy a fine. I was what the military called collateral damage.

So in her confusion, she had sought to draw me into the open. She sat on the blanket, waiting for me to come to her. She would have placed cousins and uncles and brothers in various places, watching to see what vigor I would bring to the meeting. Perhaps even Laney was somewhere nearby, he of the big hands and stained reputation.

I walked toward her. She spotted me before I'd gotten

halfway across the park, and watched me carefully as I approached. I strolled slowly with my hands in my pockets, affecting a casualness I didn't feel. An errant football bounced toward me, followed by a cry of "Little help!" from the group of teenage boys who had let it escape. I picked it up as one of them ran toward me to retrieve it, then waved him downfield for a pass, hitting him in midstride with a tight spiral that I couldn't have replicated in a hundred attempts. He crossed an imaginary goal and threw the ball down like a professional after a big score, bringing hoots from his friends. Touchdown.

When I reached the edge of her blanket, we just stared without speaking. She didn't stand and I didn't sit. For a long moment we were fixed in silent combat, until we both made silent surrenders: I looked away first and she spoke first.

"You're not going to do something foolish, are you?" she asked.

"You mean something else foolish?"

Color crept up her neck. "Don't say that. You didn't do anything wrong. At least this time." It was my turn to redden. "I needed you to be brave and noble, and you were. There's nothing foolish about that."

I squatted next to her. "No, I'm not going to do anything. At this point, I'm just curious how everything happened."

Surprise registered on her face. "You don't want to know why?"

"I'm pretty sure I know why." I looked around the park. "Are they here?"

She nodded and pointed to them.

"How are they?" I asked.

"As well as could be expected. They're glad I'm back."

"Where's Laney?"

"Still in Miami," she said. "His lawyer expects a settlement offer from the paper almost any day."

"He put that stuff in the file at the housing authority, right?"

She looked at me speculatively, her eyes as dark and fathomless as those that had stared at the camera a hundred years before. "Where do you stand in this matter?"

"What do you mean?"

"I don't mind telling you what happened. You deserve it. But once you know, what will you do?"

It was a question I had posed to myself countless times over the recent days. My allegiance to Manzini had evaporated that morning in the airport terminal in Atlanta, when I learned enough to queer their scheme but hadn't done so. And any notion I had of extracting personal compensation had likewise evaporated the moment Cooley unearthed the long-buried news story that explained the connections. So I was left with curiosity. The future was profoundly uncertain: My career was a smoking ruin, my mother was a victim that no one would believe and, for all I knew, Manzini had reported the rental car stolen and sworn a warrant for my arrest. At least I could make the past clear.

"Nothing," I said.

She didn't ask me to elaborate, which was my first hint that it all wouldn't simply end there on the blanket. "Yeah, he put the papers in the file. We'd figured out what they needed to say, and when we had them ready, he just went to the housing office one morning and said he needed to check something on his application. He just stuffed the papers in the file as he pretended to go through it and handed the whole thing to the clerk. It was back in the cabinet in minutes. No one even looked at it again 'til you asked for it."

"Did he really want to buy my apartment building?"

She nodded. "Yeah, he did. In fact, he'd already bought an option on it before we learned that's where you lived. We'd been trying to figure out how to make you write about him, and once we realized that connection already existed, everything else just fell into place."

"Why did you have to get involved?" I could hear my own bitterness. "Jesus. It's not as if a developer's never done anything illegal before. Just make an anonymous call. I'd have gotten around to the housing office eventually."

"I had to make you hate him," she said.

"Well, it worked. I do."

She then gave me my second hint. "You can stop now. You'll like him. He's big and rough-looking, but he's actually a nice guy. You know"—an odd smile crossed her face—"he sort of likes you. He says it took character for you to confront him that night. He says you were smart and cool. Got right in his face, but did it without causing a scene."

"Was that set up, too?"

She shook her head. "We'd talked about what to do if we ever ran into each other when I was with you. But we didn't orchestrate things."

"Who were those people with him?"

"A potential investor and his wife. They later decided to study other opportunities," she said dryly.

"And this lawyer in the islands?"

"A proper incorporation cost us a thousand dollars. He also agreed to confirm a few other details if anyone like you called. They have an appreciation for intrigue down there." She grinned. "Laney appropriated a few sheets of his letterhead when the lawyer's back was turned."

"How much other pretending did you do?" I may have said I wouldn't derail their scheme, but hadn't promised I wouldn't be nasty.

She didn't say anything for a long time. She watched the children play while I watched her. Finally, her gaze returned to me.

"I'm not that good an actress," she said.

We sat as the dusk deepened around us. Under the pavilion a few women stirred, folding their lawn chairs and retrieving their men from the horseshoe pit and calling their offspring into trucks. A mosquito made an exploratory orbit around my head, and as I waved it away, someone at the pavilion waved back. We were, I was reminded, the subject of scrutiny.

"How long have you known I was here?" I asked.

"A few days. How long have you been here?"

"A week," I said.

We were winding toward the inevitable question. But two other things made their way into my mind first.

"Did you nominate me?" I asked. It was an unexpected insight, a sudden connection between her careful study of me before our meeting and the mystery of my Pulitzer prize. She nodded.

"Was that part of the plan too?" I said.

"We didn't know then we'd need a plan," she answered. "I did it because I wanted to."

I moved on to the second thing. "Do you have any guesses about my mother?"

"It's pretty clear to me what happened," she said. "It's not as if she kept quiet about it." Suddenly we were on opposite sides of that great gulf, and she peered across at me pitilessly. "You were just another in a long line of men who ignored her."

I didn't want to argue, but I didn't want surrender with silence, either. "Yeah, maybe. But I didn't have the advantage of searching through my grandfather's papers."

She softened. We sat for another long, quiet moment before she finally asked it: "So what are you going to do now?"

■

I'm the designated driver.

There are not many other things I'm capable of doing. I could visit the docks and sign on as a shrimper, but being the low man on a crew is a job for someone younger, someone for whom physical labor is still exercise, not punishment. I'm presentable enough to man the front desk at the resort, but my years in journalism did little to nurture any sense of diplomacy, so I know there would come that inevitable moment when a guest's need for extra pampering would collide with my unwillingness to believe that $90 a night earns you the status of royalty. I could work for Laney, who's now building a few homes on the island, but that has all the wrong taste to it.

So I have developed a few solitary skills. I bought a crab net, then eventually two more, and have become adept at wiring raw chicken into them, weighting them properly with a smooth stone and, depending on time and tide, dropping them over one side of the pier or the other. When I pull a net back to the surface, there hopefully are at least a couple of crabs feasting on the chicken, their confusion almost palpable when suddenly the water drops away and they feel the net swinging in the air as I lift it. I am fascinated by their apparently limitless number: Do they not wonder what happened to their pals, who were here just a moment ago? . . . *Whoa! Never mind. Look what just dropped in front of me. Chicken. My favorite.*

Also, I have become a dedicated scavenger. Each dawn finds me on the beach for my daily walk, a mile up and back one morning, a mile down and back the next. I never return without a treasure. I have acquired several towels, a hooded sweatshirt, a small cooler, enough sunscreen to keep me pale for years, an almost new pair of running shoes, countless pieces of driftwood made silky by the sea and sun, and a dental bridge that now swings from the rearview mirror in my car. The two porcelain teeth have become an effective security device, something made clear the day an outlaw motorcyclist caught my eye at a traffic light in Savannah. We were suffering through a long light in adjoining lanes when I glanced toward him, prompting him to grin and pull a pair of pliers from his belt. "Hey, pardner," he said, raising his voice to be heard over the idling motorcycle, "when you get good enough at it, use these to get the real ones." He clacked the pliers menacingly several times and laughed insanely, tucking them back into his belt as the light changed. Just before he pulled away, I noticed that the four small, white objects looped together on the right side of his sleeveless denim vest were human teeth, presumably extracted from the mouths of beating victims. I may have been an amateur to him, but to the rest of the world, I later realized, anyone who can remove a dental plate from someone else's mouth is a man whose car is best left untouched.

And I drive.

The rental car is gone now, of course. I returned it to the Atlanta airport the day after my talk with Jocelyn in the park, handing the key across the counter just a few minutes before I did the same with the return ticket at the airline counter, taking care to see that its cost was credited back to the *Post-Star*. It then took me an hour to navigate the confusing maze of arrival and departure lanes and walk beyond the seemingly endless expanse of long-term parking to the highway. My first ride took me as far as Macon, leaving me to hopscotch the rest of the way to Miami over the next two days in a dozen different cars, living off rest-stop food and catching naps with my head vibrating against passenger-side windows. The last car dropped me off a block from the *Post-Star* late in the afternoon.

There were only a few things I wanted from my desk, and I briefly considered coming back later. The newsroom would be lurching toward deadline, hitting that point in the day when every hand would be on deck, and I knew my entrance then would be a spectacle. But a spectacle would be appropriate, I concluded: Hollis probably had risked his life to drag his nemesis out of some frontier saloon; my humiliation in front of dozens of acquaintances wouldn't be a modern-day equivalent, but it was as close as I was going to get.

The dread drained from me, though, with each step I took toward the building. What did I have to fear? I'd already lost what I was going to lose, and that which I'd gotten in return couldn't be taken from me, at least not by Manzini. I'd already decided to become a driver, an ambition that had been born just that morning somewhere in north Florida as I sat in a stranger's car and pondered the answer to Jocelyn's question. Nothing that happened in the newsroom would change that.

By the time I reached the *Post-Star*, I was giddy. Emile was imperturbable as ever until, as I walked by his desk in the lobby, I said loudly, "Emile! My man. What's happening, brother?" and held my palm out for a hand slap. A look of astonishment registered on his face—the first change of expression I'd ever seen—but he slapped hard as I went by. My hand tingled all the way up the elevator.

I was whistling when I entered the newsroom. One by one my colleagues fell silent as they noticed me, ending telephone conversations, halting their typing or reaching over to turn down the volume on the police scanner. The quiet was like a force field around me that dampened all sound as I walked, so when I reached my desk at the newsroom's far end, there wasn't a noise to be heard. That is, except for Manzini's footsteps as he padded up behind me.

I turned to face him. "Manzini! My man. What's happening, brother?" I said exuberantly. It had worked with Emile, so I thought I'd give it a try, although I discarded the hand slap.

Someone at a nearby desk snickered, but was cut off by a baleful look from Manzini. He then turned back to me.

"Where have you been?"

"Trying to figure out what happened," I said as I stacked my few belongings into a pile.

"You don't call or anything?" he asked, sounding more like a spurned lover than an outraged employer.

"Nothing to report."

"You've been gone more than a week. How can you have nothing to report?"

I shrugged. "Look, I did my best. I didn't find her. I've got nothing to tell you."

"We've got to file an answer with the court by tomorrow, for Christ's sake. What are we supposed to do?"

I finished rummaging through my drawers, adding the last items to the pile. "Well, you could just write Laney a check and get on with your life."

Manzini finally noticed that I was evacuating my desk. "What are you doing?" he demanded.

"I'm leaving."

"You're goddamn right you are," he said, moving quickly to get ahead of me. "Pack your things and get out." It was the essence of his leadership: Watch the parade closely and leap in front when it makes a turn.

Still, the scene had all the wrong flavor to it. Manzini may have hired me largely for the opportunity to make an easy strike on *The New York Times,* and exiled an innocent if lazy writer to Hialeah to accommodate me. But the net effect had been to provide me with the second chance I had so desperately desired. That the whole thing had been a sham was no reason now for the victims, finding no one else on the battlefield, to fight among themselves.

I stuck out my hand to shake. "Look, this was my fault in ways you couldn't even imagine. I'm sorry you got caught up in it. It had nothing to do with you."

He ignored my hand. "I hope you've got another line of work in mind."

■

I did, actually. And Manzini is still paying me.

I drive to Savannah four times a week. Each child goes once individually, then I gather them together and drive all of them for their weekly joint session. I would contribute my time and my car gladly, but Jocelyn insists on paying me, so after some inverse haggling we arrived at a reasonable compensation: a hundred dollars a week, and I had to pledge to fill the tank on her credit account at the gas station. That payment covers almost exactly the weekly rate I negotiated with Miggles for my room, and I have most of my dinners at Jocelyn's with everyone else, so I really only need a few handyman jobs a week, or one or two good mornings with my crab net, to pick up my living money. It is an altogether agreeable way to live, one that leaves me time to concentrate on driving.

I figured out the best route to the office through a prolonged trial-and-error period. We avoid the four-lane interstate entirely, instead finding our way among the state highways until we hit Savannah's southern edge. Then we weave our way through the city to the office, which is set on a side street near one of the city's statelier parks and is indistinguishable from the private homes that surround it, except for the small brass nameplate set into the brick next to the door. I usually sit in the park and read until the session is over, then retrace exactly the route home. They told me early on that rituals and predictability are valuable things.

In fact, I have added my own ritual to the process. On Friday afternoons, when the joint session is over, we stop at a little ice cream shop we discovered on one of the first trips. We all get a treat to celebrate the conclusion of another week's effort. I have pledged them to secrecy, declaring that Jocelyn would be upset at the consumption of sundaes and milk shakes just prior to dinner, and this conspiracy bonds us in a small but tangible way. I don't think she would care, actually, but she would insist on paying for it. So it is our secret.

Jocelyn and I have our own secret as well. Most of the world thinks Laney has Manzini's money, that he uses it as a salve on the wounds inflicted by the *Post-Star*. Truth be told, Laney didn't have custody of the money for more than a few weeks. Whatever was left after he paid his attorney and settled various fees and levies was wired to an account Jocelyn had established with the trust department of a Savannah bank. A collection of blue-suited, purposeful men have been given the job of massaging and kneading the money until it gives issue to well over $100,000 a year. I take a portion of that sum with me on my final trip to Savannah each week and hand it to a woman in the office where the children visit.

It isn't an office at all, in reality. It's a place of order and calm and solicitude, filled with comfortable furniture and friendly people, more like a happy grandmother's salon than a place of business. The whole operation is overseen by a serene old gentleman whose white beard and befuddled air disguise a special and expensive talent: helping three children cope with the memory of the night they watched their father saw off their mother's head.

Jocelyn is their aunt, you see, sister to a woman I had declined to help. She had gathered up the parentless children and moved them to the calm of the island, hoping that love and serenity would restore them. It helped a bit. But when it became clear that extensive, long-term therapy was needed, that love alone could not overcome the trauma, Jocelyn—applying the determination and grit honed over the generations—had set out to acquire the money to pay for it.

I do my part. I'm happy to drive and deliver payments and buy ice cream. I wait patiently as Jocelyn and I move toward that moment when I can pack my things and relocate from the motel to her home. We are feeling our way gingerly, because there is healing between us to be done, yet we have an unspoken agreement that when we think of the future, it stretches no farther than the water that surrounds us.

Like Hollis a hundred years before, I'm bound to her by both my regret and her strength.

CHAPTER
SEVENTEEN

It was always just the three of us: me, my mother and my grandfather. If there were others, I didn't know of them. I was an only child, the son of an only child and the grandson of an only child. We could have held our family reunions in a telephone booth.

There have to be others, of course. It's not possible to be that genetically isolated. So surely there are cousins scattered about, branches of the family rooted in other soils. I likely could find them if I wished. My father died before I was born, but I managed to find his mother in New York City with only a little effort. But then, perhaps that's why I've never searched for the others—she turned out to be an alcoholic who shook me down for whatever money I had in my pocket. You don't necessarily find comfort in discovery.

So we were just three. I'd like to be able tell you we were a happy little trio, living a pastoral life in rural Georgia, but it wasn't like that. I didn't like my grandfather, and I'm certain he didn't like me. He was distant and cold, a man who alternated between ignoring me and meting out punishment for every infraction of his many rules. And the rules were indeed many: how to eat, when to speak, how to do chores, when to do schoolwork, how exactly to embrace tidiness, cleanliness, God-

liness. An enormous part of my childhood was spent in the study of rules. Accommodating them all and reconciling their different demands was almost a theological exercise for me. My blessing for a strict observance of his rules was his inattention, and in those moments I achieved something close to spiritual peace.

Still, he demanded nothing of me but obedience. It was my mother who made life profoundly miserable.

Actually, she didn't create misery; rather, she became its concubine. It insinuated itself so thoroughly that it seemed to have become part of her at a molecular level. I can remember only a handful of moments when my mother seemed happy. She was occasionally wistful, especially when she talked about her brief time with my father; a few times she was reckless, such as when she found a copperhead in the garden and captured it alive, keeping it in an empty burlap seed sack for me until I got home from school and could admire it with her; and sometimes she was manic, cleaning and cooking and sassing my grandfather for several days running before retiring to her room for a long stretch. But she was hardly ever happy.

These days, of course, I'm better able to see how hard she worked to confront the cause of her unhappiness. But for most of my early life, she seemed to have an almost physical need for pity, which I gave as best I could. Later, when my supply ran out, she concocted a wild tale about a monster that had come in the night and taken a newborn child from her, apparently assuming that unhappiness rooted in things as simple as the loneliness of a remote farm and the uncertain love of a distant father would have no appeal to a wider audience. So she shopped this new tale around to whoever would listen, embellishing the details and dwelling on the horror in an effort to get somebody, anybody, to feel sorry for her. Each time she failed she went deeper into the story, so deep that eventually she became permanently disconnected from reality. Only then did she find a sort of success: the institutionalized pity of the staff of the state mental hospital.

That would have been the end of that, were it not for Jocelyn and Jack.

Jocelyn is a human, while Jack is—or was—a dog. Each of them performed a valuable task in the rehabilitation of my mother's reputation.

Jocelyn is a friend of mine, a woman of verve and tenacity. Here's what Jocelyn did: She spent the night in my grandfather's home after he died and came across a trove of letters and documents. (Verve and tenacity, it seems, can sometimes send you pawing through other people's drawers.) Idly at first, but then with growing interest, she began reading the papers, making connections between them and sorting them into a rough chronological order. As she did, something emerged from them—the suggestion that there may have been something to my mother's story. She left the papers out for me to review, which I did a few months later.

Here's what Jack did: He came to me in a dream and reminded me what he was doing the last time I saw him.

Jack was my dog when I was a child. He was a best friend during my early school years, a pretty good friend during my middle school years, and an old and lazy sort-of friend during my high school years. One day he disappeared.

At the time, my grandfather speculated that age finally had caught up with Jack as he'd foraged in the woods, and that he'd simply laid down right there for his big sleep. I didn't think about it much. I was home from college briefly, making one of what was to become increasingly rare visits, and my mother was hardly coming out of her room those days. I was beginning to understand how perfectly strange my childhood had been, so if Jack wanted to wander off somewhere and die, it was fine with me. I understood the impulse.

Jack became a memory that grew fainter by the day until,

years later, I sat and read the papers Jocelyn had excavated from my grandfather's house. A day or two after that, as I slept, Jack returned to remind me what he'd been doing just before he disappeared: digging in the garden.

My grandfather also had been digging in the garden when he died. Considering it was such a popular pastime, I eventually decided to do a little digging in the garden myself.

Jack had been kind enough to appear so vividly in my dream that I recollected exactly where in the garden he'd labored. No more than ninety minutes and three deep holes later, I found his treasure.

My grandfather's problem had been that with the passage of time, he couldn't remember exactly where he'd buried it. I can't be certain, of course, why he even felt it was necessary to look for it. Perhaps he'd gotten spooked by my mother's later letters, which had grown more and more explicit as she found the courage to explain exactly what had happened, had grown more detailed as she overcame the sense that her soiling spoke ill of her most of all. Perhaps he worried that the recipient of one of my mother's later letters himself would want to do some digging.

As it turned out, he need not have worried. No one was much interested until my shovel turned up a delicate, fist-sized skull. Then suddenly, everyone was vitally interested, even to the point of hauling a backhoe in to do in an hour what a squadron of men would need a day to accomplish. The remaining tiny bones of a human infant were found, along with a Jack-sized scattering of dog bones in another corner of the garden. A monster had indeed taken her baby, the very same monster that had planted it in her to begin with.

She had tried to tell someone about it. She had sought help and comfort in many different places. It was just her bad luck that the people she contacted were impatient, disbelieving and inured to woe. It was just her bad luck to reach out to people like me.